MID/SOUTH ANTHOLOGY

MID/SOUTH ANTHOLOGY

Edited by
CASIE DODD

BELLE POINT PRESS

Mid/South Anthology
Volume 1
© 2022 Belle Point Press, LLC
Fort Smith, Arkansas
bellepointpress.com
editor@bellepointpress.com

The acknowledgments on pp. 270–271
constitute a continuation
of this copyright page.

Edited by Casie Dodd
Design & typography by Belle Point Press

26 25 24 23 22   1 2 3 4 5

Printed in the United States of America

ISBN: 979-8-9858965-0-3

MSA01

Contents

Introduction

I grew up in a town whose name means "End of the Trail." In those days, it meant something largely different to me than it does now. Like many millennials, my suburban childhood seemed typical and uninteresting. I enjoyed "adventures" to Tulsa that usually involved shopping malls and chain restaurants. Since my family roots go pretty far back in the area, I took for granted what it was to be from Oklahoma; I never had to think about it much.

As I got older and began to make my own life decisions, like many, I felt the need to wander. Chicago became my adopted home for several years—first as a more-or-less single person, then as a newlywed and, eventually, as a new mom—in ways that I will never regret and for which I'll always be grateful. Chicago gave me space to get distance from parts of my background that had left wounds I couldn't articulate, much less confront. It allowed me the opportunity to shape a new definition of home on my own terms—a place I nearly always felt like myself, as though I belonged.

But it wasn't quite true—not entirely. During much of that time, my husband and I struggled between enjoying the opportunities in our displaced life and missing the places and people who knew us best. With our time mostly consumed by work or parenthood, we never quite found a way to build roots in Chicago beyond ourselves, which made them too shallow. I always felt like we needed more of something: more time, more stability, more chances to meet people. My own creative life slowly dried up until I thought I might quit that part of myself for good.

Then COVID happened. After all we've seen the past few years—as our culture has shifted to often hyper-local spaces trying to make sense of larger and often faraway places or forces beyond our control—I know this story isn't original, but maybe that's kind of the point. It's not very fun to have a story that's unique if no one wants to share it. As lockdown took over Chicago for a variety of reasons—mere weeks after learning I was pregnant again and in the trembling aftermath of a debilitating period of depression—I could not see a way to continue, to keep living this imaginary life. Some people leave home for good reasons. Some people find a way to rebuild and reclaim an identity that can also take root in a new community. I'm glad for them and have in some ways experienced this as well; there's a reason I still chose to settle my family in a town two hours from where I was born. But the longer I tried to deny the tug of my native region, the more I felt myself shrinking and becoming less like a person I could recognize. When the pandemic presented an opportunity for us to relocate closer to home and to start again as a growing family, by summer we had bought a house, packed up our crowded apartment, and traded Lake Michigan for the Arkansas River.

Now, two summers later, I still feel somewhat aimless, but that is largely a result of the lingering pandemic and the often-fragmentary nature of our current culture. We have a home that's still crowded, but it's surrounded by trees and hills I've known all my life. I can see family and other people I love almost any time I want. My children have accents that sound like their grandparents. I am finally where I belong, and I won't leave again.

Although I don't know all (or most) of the writers in this anthology personally, I think many of them can identify with parts of this story. Some of them have regional roots extending several generations and have never tried to leave. Some thought they had to get out but then felt the pull to return. Some wandered where they needed and then claimed a new home. On my reading, they have all found some kind of place to belong.

It's often not easy or as simple as that. Being from or living in the Mid-South can be hard to explain. Depending on the map or the context, this part of the country can be called any number of things: Southwest, Midwest, South, Southeast, South Central, Upper South. Our states share borders with many prominent regions as well as Appalachia, the Great Plains, and the "Deep South." While in some ways our central location has made our folks more eclectic and perhaps sometimes less certain about who they are (or ought to be), that does not negate the particular this-ness of this place. It reflects a resilience and adaptability that has often kept our land as strong as we are. Despite being landlocked, we are fed by rivers and lakes, nurtured by waterfalls and waves. Our hills roll in all directions; the planned burns and bonfires have a particular smell I've never found elsewhere. The overwhelming natural qualities of this region often induce our writers to explore a deep sense of place—and, frequently, the environmental concerns that come with that. That may lead some people to worship, others to despair. Family also tends to show up in our work because when you live around here, they are typically not far away.

Our *Mid/South Anthology* writers draw from many of these themes. While each piece stands on its own, I hope that together they illustrate a more cohesive vision of how we'd like to be understood. The poems, stories, and essays in this collection cover a wide range of perspectives and levels of experience: from writers just getting started to those with long-established careers. Some of our poets have very few previous publications, but we also have work by three former or current state poet laureates. Our essays feature points of view stretching across the past several decades, while the fiction takes us from the Ozarks to the Gulf. In every case, it's my hope that the writers we've given a home here help you share in the longing that comes with looking for a place of your own. Stick around and read a while. We'll be here.

Casie Dodd
Founder & Editor, Belle Point Press

Mute Moses

It was not long ago that I saw a bobcat while driving.
On Janice and highway 102, in Bethel, by the gas station
where wild peacocks are known to roam
where that day there was this queen.
Unalloyed gold her coat and eyes burgundy wine
her hips held up by torso tied tight muscle to bone,
her body lay in a grassy crag between
two gray red rocks wrapped in red clay.
Her cubs behind she guards and guides
gallantly staring startling predators circling above,
a smoke column from a brush fire lightly floats
up and out, directing something; this is God speaking.
She lies there, mute Moses, arms stretched between tides.

A Night on the Ocean

Wonder-filled whale-road, great arbiter
of white-capped waves, I saw
you dancing in the moonlight.
Mirroring proud black loons
amidst constellations tall and wide—
yet your shape remains—
at once the dancer and the dance,
the mirror and the image.
Molding grim faces to a grin
by charms folded a million
times over, wave over wave over.
Reticent rapscallion of red and gold
coral and fishes and seals gray and gold in sunlight,
chorus humming from hypnotic
faces of blues and purples,
the deeps contained in common
with night sky, the moon's companions,
painted with unsteady hand, dancing.
To look in is to gaze out and up and down.
To touch is to live all over again,
all life jitters just under our skin,
and dipping down but to sip, we drown.

Apple

Even now when I place one
in my child's hand, and it perfectly fills
a five-year-old hand, I see the apples
dug day after day from the bottom
of that hospital bag, a shapeless sack
brought back to me from a friend's travels
because I'd never seen much of anything
outside of Tennessee.

The same bag I rolled clean swaddles
into for my sick baby, the muslin washed
carefully at home so they'd smell like home,
slept with close to my chest where the baby
should be, so they would smell like me.

Jazz and Pink Lady when I could find them,
always sunk to the depths of the cotton.
Tossed in only so I could hold her all day
without rising, one arm with her head resting
on it, the other crooked so I could eat
with one hand. If I remembered to eat,
I ate them bruises and all.

The Work of Breathing

I.

Honest, necessary,
the pull and release,

slow swell and lift,
air heavier than water,

than snow in mid-winter,
sucked in. The ribs heave,

her chest shrugs off the cold disk
of stethoscope, and cardiologists

listening to the language of the heart
which she speaks so poorly,

mispronouncing the simplest phrase.

II.

I look at the wall where there was once a clock
and find more time there than before.

III.

The students gather around us,
mother and child in the ICU.

We both wear Madonna blue.
May we listen? The teacher asks,

I unwrap the onesie from her chest
while she sleeps the sleep of one

who has worked a double-shift,
and has another coming. Each takes

a turn pressing his ear to marvel
at the death talking quietly there.

The Isle of Grief

We were already alone. Everyone could see us
from miles off, but we stopped trying
to communicate—first letting go
of the fires, the smoke signals, the twigs
spelling out our needs. We changed
to suit our environment, learned to make do
with what we were provided.

I wove a dress of vine and birdfeather, all black.
Turning earthward, you dug down until fresh water
pooled like a memory in cupped hands.

Still, there was always hunger, a wanting
buried deep in the belly. I looked for her
outline on the shore, blurred with distance,
haze of heat and water, but sometimes I could see her
hair color on another, then the exact size of her body.

We stopped standing on that shore.
No one could cross unless they were taken,
or someone was taken from them.

ELI CRANOR

One Bad Mother

ELLOYWEEN JUDKINS had long gray hair all the way down past her ass braided tight and tied back with a leather barrette at the tip. Big black snow goose feather stuck in there too, holding it all together. Made Jackson think of this elephant he'd seen online, had a brush in his trunk, slapping paint up against a white wall at some zoo in Africa, or maybe Baltimore. Jackson couldn't remember, but he could still see his aunt standing guard over her new cash register. The one with the card reader she'd bought for the firework stand on Highway 124, just a couple miles short of Gum Log, Arkansas, the same stand she'd been running for going on damn near two decades now.

Jackson's daddy—Aunt Elly's brother—said his sister made enough dough from June 15 through July 10 to live a halfway decent life the rest of the year. "She lives like a gypsy hiding out in that tent all damn summer," Darrel Judkins had said when Jackson came around asking about the job. "Or some sort of witch doctor from over in Eastern Oklahoma. That's where she met that Indian knocked her ass up. A shaman or some shit for the Muscogee Creek Nation."

Jackson took the job the next day, and Aunt Elly told him basically the same thing minus the part about the shaman knocking her up. Said the gig was harder than it looked, hot as hell too, but the trick was always having a bucket of water handy, shifting her eyes toward a red tin bucket hanging from a pole in the far back corner.

What the old woman hadn't said, though, was anything about needing "help." Just told her teenage nephew she'd pay him minimum wage, eleven bucks an hour for as many hours as he could work over the twenty-six-day span.

Jackson slapped at his neck, and his fingers came back wet and bloody. Rolled what was left of the dead mosquito into a ball and flicked it in the direction of his aunt, same way he would a booger. Elloyween didn't seem to notice, too busy standing guard over that register.

Twenty-five straight days and Jackson had rarely seen her move. Thirty, maybe forty words had been shared between them after that first talk. Elloyween kept an RV out back, couple hundred feet to the east of the lime-green camping tent she'd pitched after her nephew agreed to her terms and conditions. Four collapsible poles and a thin sheet of polyester: Jackson's only escape from the baking heat and his aunt's hazy blue eyes, watching him as she rang up a meth-mouthed woman, glancing over the lady's bony shoulders to the nearly empty crate of smoke bombs on the middle row of card tables, telling her nephew to get his ass to work without saying a word.

It had taken Jackson twenty-five days, seventeen pallets of fire-works, and probably over a thousand customers to come up with his plan. Of the few words his crazy old aunt had spoken during that time, one of them was "Twice."

That was the response Elloyween had given the boy after he'd finally worked up the nerve to ask if she'd ever been robbed. Didn't tell him how much had been taken, or if anybody'd gotten hurt, just held up two crooked fingers—each one laced with a couple turquoise rings—and said, "Twice." Jackson had swallowed and waited for more, but his aunt didn't budge, staring back at him from behind her fancy new register like some old stone-faced Indian chief.

Dumbass goose feather, Jackson thought, unloading a fresh pack of smoke bombs onto the card table, watching his aunt ring up Meth Mouth. He'd seen family portraits from back when his dad was a kid, a little redheaded girl always tucked in next to him. Weren't many redheaded Indians, as far as Jackson knew. That damn goose feather was an act like everything else. One big show the crazy old coot was putting on, trying to come off tough because she was alone. Stuck out in that tent every summer for going on twenty years, guarding her register, all that money she had stuffed in there.

Had to be twenty, maybe thirty grand, and Jackson was looking at getting a check for less than a thousand bucks once it was all said and done. What's worse, Elloyween wouldn't pay him one red cent until the tent was packed up, the three-hundred-foot-long sucker that made Jackson think of elephants again. Some dusty-ass circus. Aunt Elly the ringleader, bossing her little clown around, making Jackson do all the work, hauling so many damn boxes his forearms locked up and his back throbbed in the night. He'd tried sleeping in the green tent she'd set up for him but couldn't do it. Started coming in later, leaving earlier as the days dragged on, what little money the dingbat had offered him withering away at both ends.

Somehow, though, he'd made it through to *the* end. Tonight was the last open night. Tomorrow was reserved for cleanup.

Meth Mouth slid a card into the chip reader. Jackson squinted, narrowing his eyes on the register's electronic display. Three-hundred-and-forty-seven dollars. The boy's jaw went slack, his mouth hanging partway open when his aunt's blue eyes cut over at him. Jackson mumbled and turned away, quick, unable to believe anybody'd pay that much dough for fireworks six days after the Fourth of July.

Meth Mouth slinked her way out through the tent's front flap, fingers holding tight to the four plastic bags stuffed full of explosives. Jackson watched her, wondering where she was going and how she'd get there. He hadn't seen a car.

It was getting late. Almost time to start cleaning up, especially considering all the fireworks that were left over. Elloyween kept a surplus of the good stuff—cases of Excalibur artillery shells, a couple boxes stuffed full of five-hundred-gram multi-shot finale cake, fireworks with names like "One Bad Mother" and "Gorilla Warfare." Took Jackson a while to realize his aunt just kept whatever was left over each year and sold it for the same price the following season. It was enough to make him start thinking, coming up with his master plan.

Jackson said, "Gotta take a piss," without looking back, already headed for the tent's south flap. Didn't even stop when his aunt said, "Be careful, Jackson." Slowed him down some, the tender-sounding sentiment catching him off guard, not quite sure what to make of it. Like he couldn't take a piss on his own all of a sudden?

Except Jackson wasn't going to take a piss and *that's* what had him worrying. Made him step a little lighter across the dry red clay, hustling through the dark for the lime-green tent and the couple thousand bucks worth of artillery shells he had holed away in there.

* * *

Elloyween eyed the red bucket hanging from the tent's southeastern pole. All the years she'd spent under that canopy and she'd never had to use it. Yet the bucket remained.

Not a fire extinguisher. A bucket. Fire extinguishers had too many parts. Too many knobs to turn and levers to pull. Things could get hot quick in a firework stand. Elloyween learned this the hard way. No, there'd never been any fires, but she had been robbed twice, just like she'd told the boy. Both experiences changed her, sharpened her skills in different ways.

What she learned the first time was that setting up a perimeter was necessary. Every night, for twenty-six straight nights, she'd forced herself to walk the premises holding a Maglite way up high beside her face, the way a cop carries one, shining the beam into bushes and behind trees. What you didn't want was anybody getting inside the tent and getting an armload of roman candles.

That's what had happened the second time, Elloyween standing there with her granddaddy's double barrel, holding it low at her hip because the kid was right *there*, grinning at her like he knew she wasn't going to pull the trigger.

Elly didn't have any qualms about shooting a thief—not after John Crowe Blackstone had opened her eyes all those years ago, casting his spell on her out back of the Cherokee Casino and Hotel in Roland, Oklahoma, leaving a part of himself inside her, a part she couldn't protect no matter how many lessons she'd learned—but she still couldn't pull that trigger. And that's when she learned the second lesson.

Which was simple: You can't shoot a shotgun—or any sort of firearm, for that matter—inside a firework stand. The kid with the armload of roman candles got away with about forty bucks worth of product, and Elloyween got a Baikal 4611, a nasty-looking little snub-nosed pistol that fired rubber bullets using a single CO_2 cartridge. Whole damn cartridge every time you pulled the trigger. Packed a punch without causing a spark. No fire. Nothing that might set off the highly volatile contents inside Elly's red-and-white-striped tent.

The two robberies had taught her well and cost her relatively little, all things considered. The air gun ran her a couple hundred bucks and was strapped to the underside of the card table, directly beneath her new register. She touched it from time to time, probably once every thirty minutes, just to make sure the Velcro strap she'd screwed into the cracked plywood was holding.

It was.

The gun felt lighter than a real gun, something like a toy, but it was enough. The perfect tool for the job, if it came to that. The only wild card was her nephew.

Jackson's presence worried Elloyween, made her upper lip tremble and sweat. She knew what her brother Darrel was doing sending the kid her way, but Jesus, it'd been so long. And the boy wasn't much help anyway. A slacker, that's what he was. Always moping around the tent, getting there later and later each morning. It pained Elloyween to see how sorry he was. How pitiful Darrel had let him become.

Elloyween ran her fingertips over the air gun strapped beneath the table, picking at it like a dried piece of bubble gum, a scab that wouldn't heal, knowing better than to blame her brother for how the boy'd turned out. An image of John Crowe Blackstone in his black leather vest and jeans—a choker with an eagle's wing bone tied to it wrapped tight around his neck—flashed over the creases of Elly's mind. There for a moment then gone. Replaced by the boy, pushing his way through the tent's back fold, bent over at the waist but straightening as he entered. Smiling too. A sly grin that reminded her so much of his father it hurt.

Elly slid her fingers off the air gun, finding purchase on the register instead. It was late. A little past midnight. The tent empty, just like it would remain for another long year. It was finally here, the moment they'd both been waiting for: closing time.

The register chimed as the drawer slid open. That got the boy's attention. She pushed the drawer shut again, trying to ignore Jackson's prying eyes, probably wondering about that feather in her hair, all those rings she always wore.

"Jackson Lee?" Elly said. "It's time we had us a talk."

Jackson said, "The time for talking's over," and raised both hands.

The silver Zippo had a skull on the front wearing a do-rag, two hollow black eyes peeking out over Jackson's left index finger, his thumb hovering a half inch over the flint wheel. Elly didn't see the long run of fuse in the boy's right hand, but it was there, curling out the bottom of his fist, marking a path behind him, a trail of black powder wrapped in asphaltum, the green water-proofing agent that always reminded Elloyween of hoses she'd drunk from as a child.

Elly didn't have to see the fuse to know what was happening. She knew this day would come. She'd been waiting for it, the same way she'd been waiting for John Crowe Blackstone to come riding back into her life on that cobalt-blue Harley with the ape-hanger handlebars. Elloyween closed her eyes and tried picturing the man after almost twenty years, imagining the gray in his thick black hair, the crow's feet marking the corners of his eyes, when Jackson said, "Empty that register, Elloyween. I ain't telling you again."

Lighter fluid always reminded Elly of the airport, that one time she'd flown out of Little Rock all the way down to south Texas hunting up her medicine man, wanting to tell John the news. But there'd been no signs of the so-called shaman by the time she'd arrived. No tracks left along the River Walk. Still, the smell remained, lodged in Elloyween's nostrils as she opened her eyes and finally saw the fuses, a whole bunch of them knotted together, snaking their way behind the boy over the hard-packed dirt before disappearing under the tent's back flap.

"*Jackson.*" That was all Elloyween could think to say, so she'd said it, not liking her tone at all.

The boy said nothing, inching his fists closer together.

"Whatever you got waiting at the end of them fuses," Elly tried, "ain't worth what I got in this register. Can promise you that."

"I got enough artillery shells and finale cake back there to blow this tent to Tijuana. Now, open that goddamn register."

Elly almost whispered his name again but refrained. She'd gone this long without scolding the boy. Why start now?

"I'll open the register," Elly said, sliding her fingers back under the table again, finding the Baikal's coarse black grip, "but I'd like to talk to you first, Jackson. Tell you why Darrel really sent you out here to spend the summer with me."

The boy said, "I's the one went to him asking about the job," the Zippo's orange flame standing straight up under the stuffy tent. "Daddy ain't got nothing to do with it."

Elloyween held tight to the air gun strapped beneath her new cash register, still hoping she wouldn't have to use it but unable to ignore the look in Jackson's eye. The same feral expression that had called to her all those years ago in the casino's parking lot, the Harley's two-cylinder, piston engine howling out its siren's song, a low growl that had rattled Elly's thighs on up into her heart, leaving her numb when the motorcycle ride was over and it was John Crowe Blackstone's turn.

"Your daddy . . ." Elloyween whispered then shook her head. "I mean, no. This ain't about him. It's about you and me—"

*Ho*ly shit," Jackson said and touched the flame to the fuse. "Been stuck in this hell hole with you for a month. A whole damn month"—the fuse crackled to life—"and you ain't said shit about nothing. *Nothing*."

The fountain of sparks flickered down the cord, almost to Jackson's bony knuckles, when he dropped it. Elloyween watched the fuzzy yellow fireball whizz between his feet, running the numbers in her head. She'd been in the business long enough to know professional-grade fuses—the big thick green ones—traveled about a half second per foot.

"Jackson Lee Judkins," she said and straightened, surprised at how easily she'd assumed a mother's scalding tone. "We got fifteen, maybe twenty seconds before that tent out back goes up like the Challenger." The boy's nose scrunched and Elly had to remind herself of his age, how young he was, younger still than she'd been that night in Roland, Oklahoma. "What I'm saying," Elly said and slapped the register, "this here's a new model. Got one them fancy chip readers and everything."

The boy shrugged as the fuse rushed out of the tent.

"There ain't no *money*," Elly said. "Jesus Christ. Everything's gone digital. Got a couple hundred bucks worth of cold cash in these drawers. Everything else is already in the bank."

Jackson's eyes widened in a way that John Crowe Blackstone's would've never done. Elly couldn't help but wonder if that was his mother coming out in him. The question worried her but didn't last long, replaced by that fuse still sparkling out there somewhere, getting awfully damn close to that lime-green tent.

Jackson said, "Shit," and dropped the Zippo. "What're we gonna do?"

Elly knew the answer. It was something she'd learned a long time ago, a lesson she'd held close to her heart for when things got tough. Her eyes darted to the back-left corner of the tent and Jackson turned, then started sprinting, making a beeline for the bucket.

Elly smiled to herself, proud he'd at least learned that much, a lesson about life and being prepared, or something. Elly wasn't sure if there was any greater meaning other than it was just nice to have a bucket of water handy when you run a firework stand. Elloyween was so busy watching the boy—the way his legs flailed sideways as he ran, bowlegged just like his daddy—she didn't notice the bucket dancing beneath its wire handle, jerking this way and that. But she could still feel the Baikal's grip beneath the table, that Velcro strip holding tight, and found herself picking at one corner as Jackson Lee pushed through the tent's back flap and into the night.

* * *

A kiddie song. That's what was playing on repeat in Jackson's mind, the red bucket clanking against the boy's left knee as he ran. The same knee he'd cut wide open on the big green slide his last year at Dwight Elementary. Sign outside the school had an Indian chief painted on it, full headdress, the works. Made Jackson feel funny for some reason. Same way he'd felt all summer working for Elloyween.

He was feeling different now, though. The way Aunt Elly'd stared at him, her soft, strange tone of voice, a humming sound in Jackson's mind, humming the tune to that children's song he'd learned his first year at Dwight, coming back to haunt him. No. That wasn't right. *Warn* him. Yeah. An old man singing with his aunt's voice about a hole.

Jackson looked down and saw red dirt through the half-dollar-sized hole in the bucket, the fuse a dark green snake caught in the crosshairs. The sparks shot past beneath the bucket and Jackson jumped, following the fireball with his eyes.

The lime-green tent was up another fifteen, maybe twenty feet, but Jackson wouldn't let his eyes get that far ahead of him. He was just a boy, and whatever Elly'd been saying to him earlier—or trying to say—it had stirred new questions deep inside his heart. More than anything, he did not want to die.

The bucket clanked at Jackson's feet, and the boy squeezed both eyes shut, waiting to feel the fire on his face, that small flame that had flickered to life all those nights ago in Oklahoma, the spark Jackson knew nothing about but carried inside him always. He still wasn't ready for it but figured if you had to go out early, you might as well go out with a bang. A grand fuckin' finale, man . . .

A single, soft *pop*.

Like a tire blowing out in a storm, the sound muffled by the rain. It wasn't raining out back of Elloyween Judkin's firework stand, and Jackson wasn't dead either.

The boy's eyes opened, the left one first followed by the right, blinking for a bit then going straight for the lime-green tent, tracing the charred remains of the burned-out fuse through the front flap, surprised to find darkness—only darkness—waiting inside.

The meth-head woman had a grocery cart.

Elly heard the wheels plowing through the gravel. Steel on stone, scraping. She turned and saw the mounds of finale cake, glittering boxes and tubes, gunpowder packed down tight in there, pounds and pounds of it. Enough to blow the tent to Tijuana, just like Jackson had said. Enough to make it real damn hard to push that cart through the gravel.

Elloyween lifted the Baikal out to one side and pulled the trigger with a certain nonchalance, her body language tired and whispering, "Goddamn it. God*damn* it." The rubber bullet hit the woman dead center in the back, right between her knobby shoulder blades. The meth head stumbled but did not go down, knees wobbly for a moment until she steadied herself against the cart's plastic handle.

The sound of the Baikal echoed through the pines, that soft *pop* mocking Elloyween again and again. A toy. That's what the air gun felt like now. And the woman, she just kept going, getting farther and farther away.

The meth head made it to the highway and disappeared around a bend just as Jackson stepped out from behind the edge of the tent, still holding that red bucket in his hands. Elloyween listened to his footsteps in the dark. She let him come up right beside her, close enough she could feel his heat. Could smell him too. So different than it'd been before, back when he was tiny and had just come out.

Elly stared down the long dark road, picturing that poor woman and her grocery cart out there somewhere, wondering, maybe, if she could've been Elloyween in another life, if Elly could've been her had things gone different with the medicine man.

Easter

sunflowers Jesus came back marigolds
instead of man Jesus rose petal bleeding
heart vine lamb's ear listening the wind
beggar going on I make all things new
the firewood green with moss forgiving
the clover breaking it open as it will
forgive the flame sometimes an angel asks
for tenderness but of Mary he needed
tinder she broke open like firewood
no like a sunflower craning its head up
pray God never needs me too many
of the saints had no choice the trials hotter
than the June a stranger found me on my
face rolled me over all I saw was sky

Christmas

Gray again. The kind of wind it takes
to strip one flag, sew another.
Wring your hair. Toss your harp. Humid
what the morning lit. A noel no. A howl.
One train rusting the horizon in half.
A nest among the low branches. Defeat too
has its crowns. Air at the lake is good
for the lungs, but you are a stranger among
its smells. Up/past. Reach across. This
field. Everything beneath it will be upturned
when the kingdom comes back. Ready
the plow. Bathe. Your best honey for parable.
What burns determines the scent of its smoke.
What burns longer. We buried ours today.

Geographies

I.

My tongue has come to know the thistle and its pairing with
vinegar and pepper and the itch surrounding watery eyes
upon bringing goldenrod up to the nose.

I have exhausted all I have to say and I have known so little
here—how the river came to be locked in place is just a story
told over plate lunches. I know no more and no less.

II.

> The poem, yes, the poem, roams where unsweet-
> ened callings demand. It traverses the back porch
> freshly washed after gutting sac a lait, the flat
> bottom of the pirogue drying beside the pond,
> the cow tongue stewing in the Christmas lunch
> Magnalite, and I have rewritten the ending
> sentence because I do not want to go there. Not
> right now. Not with the house in its current state
> after the storm, not with the port being placed
> within the body for treatment. See, the port is
> debated and delegated. The port is intentional.

III.

A man canoed the entirety of the Mississippi River and feared the might of barges and ocean liners when he neared Venice. Suddenly, I am docked watching the bridge open over Bayou Dularge as a tugboat blasts its carnival horn upon my request. It is easy to be dwarfed as a child, easy to be made small when a category five has a width of 300 miles. It is flatland here. I pretend distant clouds are mountainscapes.   We are in search of our size.

Ida, 23

I must have been the only car headed east,
the only fool headed towards the dirty side
of the storm. How did you come to be named?

> My grandmother can't remember why she
> left their home, but she knows which way
> those winds turn to extend its breath upon us.

We sit around the TV and watch your temper
build for days over places where water is clear—
everything breathes when you move through.

> Garage doors expand and contract like the cragged
> animal body of a horse and trees bow for prayer
> of a swift passing and no water lines.

TAYLOR GREENE

Force

The river plains of Arkansas
stretch to the horizon, the pines
break apart the endless cloud-topped
fields of crops, hiding the Ozarks
that you know you can reach out
and grab, only if your move your fingers
to the north, only if you can tell
apart the mountains and the mounds
of mud-stained cotton, piled next to
the wind-swept tree, branches pointing
you to the end of Miller County Road 8.

The river is miles from you,
standing in this empty cotton field,
the river sculpted this place, not like
the glacial plains of the Midwest, formed
in the slow global push of ice across
the surface, the river levels in anger
flooding the land time and time again,
breathing life into the soil, leveled
again by machines breathing fire found
deep below the same ground they till.

Blue

I'd like to tell you of a January day:
bright, Mississippi cotton
clouds hanging lazy
in a haint blue sky;
on the porch she
hung white sheets
glowing in the sun,
phantoms waltzing with the wind.

CASSIE E. BROWN

Thawing

WHEN JACKIE NEIMEYER walked into the bookstore, she was startled to see Bobcat Pope. She couldn't have been more surprised, in fact, if her head had fallen off.

She had always known Robert. Their families' farms had been near to each other, and she remembered he was always as kind as a rough farm boy could be. In fact, she had once dated him, when they were in school together in Nowhere—her three years behind him—but she hadn't laid eyes on him since the night she graduated in 1981. Jackie had earned a scholarship to the University of Missouri in Kansas City and had left in the fall of that year.

She never expected to see him again, having long ago bid good riddance to the town, made up of a collection of houses, four churches, a school, a few assorted businesses, and an auction barn.

Nowhere had been a tough place to grow up gay.

Of course, Jackie had told no one what she was. She had been silent and secret. She had dated guys, like Bobcat, throughout school, starting in junior high. She had dated guys who were cocky on the basketball court, but shy and gentle when alone. She had dated the ones who demanded nothing more from her than to look as pretty as she could in awkward heels at the senior dance, with the puffy shoulders of a peach-colored prom dress up around her ears. She had always danced backwards in Nowhere, turning in circles, spinning in place.

She never allowed her gaze to linger long on the girls who fueled her fires. The hard and swearing jock girls. The delicate bookish girls, thin like ghosts with fear behind their glasses.

And, of course, Anna. Anna was her own animal. She was a country hick, with words slow around the edges. Anna's accent stumbled over words like "theorem" and "judiciary," but she aced tests anyway. It was hard to pin words on Anna, and Jackie only ever described Anna in her mind with possessive phrases, telling what Anna owned. Anna's contagious laughter. Anna's Ford pick-up. Anna's tender heart. Anna's kindness. Anna owned Jackie too, though Jackie never said so.

More than the prom dresses and rough farm boys, the ignorance and the too-tight families, it was Anna who had helped Jackie escape to the tiny bars with the pink triangles. It was Anna who drove her to find her Sapphic sisters in Judy's Place, an alley bar bursting with three high-top tables, a dance floor, and a jukebox spinning Joan Jett and the Blackhearts, the Bee Gees, and once in a while, Patsy Cline. Of course, only Patsy sounded like home to Jackie. It was at Judy's where she first danced with another woman.

Judy's had been her refuge from streets that smelled like cars and concrete, not prairie. When Judy's folded, as all lesbian bars are wont to do, she found Lil's. When Lil's changed ownership and became a sports bar filled with straight people, the city was then entirely without a lesbian bar, and she was forced to find Her Garden—a women's bookstore, full of women's history, women's activist literature, and women with short hair and lengthy agendas. There was no dance floor to spin on here, just Tuesday night poetry readings. Her Garden was home to radical feminist politics and bad haircuts.

She presumed Bobcat Pope shared only the haircut, as she had known him as a Reagan man. In his good denim and his Red's Tractor Supply cap, he looked lost, and her initial wave of fear gave way to a strange sort of pity.

"Bobcat?" she ventured finally, as she stepped up behind him. "Bobcat Pope, is that you?"

When Bobcat turned to Jackie, his eyes took a moment to focus, as if he were hearing something far away. Instead of needing to call out a thousand yards across a field of soybeans, however, he found himself right alongside Jackie, as near as he had ever been, he thought, to a lesbian.

He finally ventured to say her name. "Jackie? Jackie Neimeyer?"

"Yeah, it's me," she responded.

It was Tuesday night, and the store was becoming more crowded, and one of the clerks, Jonna, was clearing her throat dangerously close to the slim standing mic. Then there was a restless silence in the audience, and Jackie watched Bobcat's face. It was just about thirteen years since she had last laid eyes on him, and those years had gone to his eyes. It was more than the prematurely graying hair. It was more than the crow's feet etched by farming in the sun. There was something unfamiliar about the darkness that hung in the air around him.

"Welcome to Her Garden!" declared Jonna in a cheerful voice, and as the crowd of women gave spirited shouts, Bobcat startled.

"It's Tuesday night," Jackie explained to him. When this provoked more confusion than it alleviated in his expression, she smiled. "Let's go," she said, "There's a coffee shop around the corner. I'm buying."

He nodded, and followed mutely out, bumping into each and every one of the folding chairs between the back of the store where they stood and the door. He drew the ire and suspicion of each woman he nudged. He kept his eyes on Jackie's back, stepping only where she had stepped, as if he were a child afraid of becoming separated. He knew he was simply unwelcome and could not figure out how to apologize for his presence. He fleetingly hoped his mama would forgive his lapse in manners.

It was a rainy late March, and the smell of concrete and cars had washed off the streets. Bobcat drew a deep breath as he stepped into a puddle on the sidewalk in his best Justin cowboy boots. He followed Jackie as she walked the two blocks toward the Sunflower Cafe.

The coffee shop had its cheery namesake painted on the glass windows. Bobcat had never seen more descriptions for coffee in his life. A "coffee shop" to him was a place where your options were "leaded and unleaded," as Barb, his favorite waitress at the Circle M, always said so brightly. A coffee shop was a place where you could get a piece of pie with your coffee around 10:00 a.m. His favorite was coconut cream. In Nowhere, the coffee shop across the street from the auction barn offered big farmer's breakfasts. The Sunflower's heaviest offering seemed to be a muffin, and a rather scrawny one in his opinion. He skipped the muffin and allowed Jackie to order for him—"Two plain coffees, large, please." Bobcat reached into the back of his Wranglers to pull out his wallet, but Jackie stopped him with a gentle hand. She reached into her own back pocket and pulled out five ones, and she walked off from the register with two large china mugs of steaming coffee.

Bobcat took a sip, and decided the coffee tasted a little weird. But then he began to wonder if it was just the whole situation that was weird, and the coffee was just fine. He took another sip and realized that Jackie had said nothing to him since they had arrived but was watching him intently.

He didn't quite know where to begin, so he panicked a little, and started in the middle.

"Anna's sick."

"Anna?" Jackie's tongue felt thick in her mouth.

"Anna Martin. She was in your class," Bobcat trailed off. He began to list the ways she might remember Anna, as if reciting from the 1981 edition of the Nowhere, Missouri, J. C. Nolan High School yearbook: "She pitched softball? She was our FFA treasurer? She was nominated for prom queen, but she didn't win." His recitation began to wander off course. "I mean, nobody thought she'd win. I still can't figure out who in the hell nominated her—"

"I did."

"Oh. So you remember Anna?"

"I never forgot her," Jackie responded. And Bobcat couldn't quite figure out what that meant or if she sounded angry. He had always been more comfortable with animals than men, and men than women. Women were a distant, inscrutable third.

"If you thought I would have forgotten her, why the fuck would you drive all the way to Kansas City to tell me this?" He flinched at her easy profanity but was now confident that she was angry.

"I talked to your mom, and she told me where you were," he said.

"But why?"

"Because she wanted you to know!" Bobcat tried not to raise his voice.

"My mom?" Jackie spat the word.

"No! Anna! It was Anna who wanted you to know."

This shocked Jackie into silence for only a moment, as one question rose to the surface above the troubled whirl in her mind.

"How did you know I'd be at Her Garden?"

Bobcat blushed a little. "I didn't. I guessed. Your mom told me you were . . . that you are—"

"A lesbian?" Jackie said, and something in her tone was like a coonhound growling over its food.

"Yeah."

"And you just happened to know that all lesbians go to Her Garden on Tuesday nights?"

Bobcat dropped his voice so low she had to lean forward to hear him, as he muttered, "Chris told me."

"Chris who?" Jackie asked.

"My cousin."

She had never seen Chris Pope at any of the paltry host of city functions at which Kansas City's gays and lesbians gathered, but she knew that Bobcat would never tell a lie to bring shame on the Pope family. And being gay in Nowhere was surely a source of shame.

Jackie had somehow believed she was the only gay person to ever come from Nowhere. The only one who had ever suffered in silence. The only one whose life had been consumed with lies and secrecy. The revelation that destroyed this myth of isolation was entirely too much. And Anna . . .

Jackie fought the tears that began rolling, but she couldn't fight them long.

When Jackie arrived at Nolan Regional Hospital, twenty-three miles from Nowhere, she realized her breathing had become shaky, and she calmed herself as best she could. It was raining again—the kind of cold, hard spring rain full of threats and promises. She had seen patches of daffodils in the front yards of the citizens of Nolan and Nowhere. The world was thawing from a nasty cold snap, and the daffodils—the tiny, hardy bits of sunshine—were poking blossoms through a light dusting of snow. The rain would melt the rest. She had been unhappy with the weather's recent turn, as the early morning drive from Kansas City had taken her across myriad creeks and minor rivers, and all hung thick with fog.

Driving back from Kansas City, she had seen the changes. From the highway she had seen more houses than she had recalled. The suburbs stretched out further, with their outlet malls, chain restaurants, and subdivisions. Then she left the interstate. Lettered and numbered county roads were now lined with clusters of houses as well. The city seemed to haunt her, calling her back home, always at her back. As the sun rose, bringing the fog up from the creeks, she saw something else new. She knew the rolling hayfields, standing empty in the winter, with cattle huddled together. She knew the ancient, graying hay barns, leaning sideways away from the prevailing winds. This had been her world once, as a horse-crazy girl. But the long, low gray tin roofs of the corporate chicken barns—their sharp stench filling the air—these were an ugly sort of progress.

She had driven in early in the morning and had barely gotten out of the innermost tangle of the city's suburbs when she realized what a bad idea that was. On foggy mornings, in the strange, pink-tinged darkness before the daybreak, deer would be out. It was dangerous driving. The time would change next week, and then she would have been driving in daylight. She would have had the opportunity to drive faster, with less fear.

But she hadn't had the time.

Anna's cancer had progressed pretty far, according to Bobcat. He provided no details. She had not asked. In Kansas City, she had grown accustomed to hearing lengthy reports on illnesses when people she knew were hospitalized, with loved ones parroting lists of symptoms and long diagnoses that they would have been hard pressed to explain.

In Nowhere, Anna was simply dying.

Anna was at Nolan Regional—because it was close to home, not because it was well regarded. From her high school days, Jackie remembered stories of people with the wrong legs amputated there by doctors who could no longer practice in other states, and she didn't know if they were untrue. It was the county hospital and served its purpose, she supposed. Jackie had been born there, which meant the first day or so of her life was spent in a town, but very little of her childhood had followed suit.

Jackie drew a deep, cold breath and got out of her car. As she walked into the hospital, she felt like the hay barns, falling forward away from the wind. It was difficult to walk, and she found the oncology wing with a little help from the nurses. She had walked into the wrong wing at first, of course. She turned left instead of right and had to meander back through the emergency room to find her way back to the desk. As she got closer to the hospital room, she found herself walking faster and faster, as if all of Nowhere were hiding around each corner, ready to wreak vengeance.

Then she was with Anna Martin at last.

When Jackie walked in, Anna was asleep, and she was uncertain if she should try to wake Anna or not, so she looked to the ravaged, rough-looking man, Hank Martin, who was Anna's father. Hank was tall and lanky and had been living out of Anna's hospital room for the past three weeks. He went home and showered, as he could, but had not done so in two days as Anna had worsened, and he smelled like it. Jackie was caught sideways by the smell of Stetson cologne gone sour, and sweat, and some sort of bleach cleaner, and urine, and the unmistakable smell of sickness under it all. She tried desperately not to retch. When Anna's father looked at her though, she became more self-conscious than queasy.

She knew what she must look like in his eyes.

Her hair was cut short and masculine, just as she always asked from Barry at the Royal City Barbershop. She never wore makeup and had not put any on just to make nice; she now regretted this. She had opted for a muted forest green and pink plaid flannel men's shirt, under her Levi's jean jacket which was covered with buttons emblazoned with slogans (Womyn Unite!), from marches and protests (ACT UP!), and her favorite, a pink triangle with the black double-headed axe of the labrys on it. It was the symbol of the Minoan goddess cultures, she had been told: a symbol of womyn's power. Her boots were a long-abused pair of black Doc Martens. Yes, she knew what she must look like in his eyes.

His eyes were sharp and seemed to have missed not a lick in their appraisal. He took her in quickly, like sizing up an early weaned calf. "Jackie, it's nice to see you," Mr. Martin managed, with more warmth than she expected, after taking it all in. "I know Anna missed you, and we're really glad you've come home."

"Nice to meet you, Mr. Martin." She held her hand out, like a man would, and Mr. Martin did not hesitate. His hand was rough, with callouses across the palms that felt as if they would cut her open. They were farmer's hands; they were her father's hands.

Surrounded by the hospital stink, the beeping of machines, held tightly within the warm grasp of Mr. Martin's hands, Jackie felt all of her armor fall away. It was armor she needed, built by years of separation, and the lack of it made her cry. "*Home,*" he had said, "*you've come home.*"

"It's okay," he said, and he pulled the strange girl into his arms. She was a child, and he was a father, and in that moment that was what mattered most. So they cried together, mingling their grief wordlessly.

"Jackie?" The voice was so pitifully weak, and yet it crashed into their moment.

"Anna!" Hank Martin let Jackie go, and nodded to her, as Jackie crossed the two steps of the small room to the hospital bed. She sat in the chair beside Anna's head, and the two of them looked at each other. Jackie remembered Anna's cheeks as smiling and round with baby fat. Now they were sunken and pale. Jackie remembered Anna's eyes as sparkling and brown. Now they were flat and dull as old pennies. But when she whispered Jackie's name again in her kitten-weak voice, Jackie smiled radiantly.

"I'm here," Jackie answered.

"Good," Anna said, and a ghost of her old smile crossed her lips. "I needed you . . . here . . . you know." In between phrases, her voice wheezed, and at the end she nearly coughed.

"You needed me?" Jackie repeated, confused.

"You never forget . . . your first . . . love," Anna continued, "And I've never . . . forgotten . . . you."

Jackie glanced up in fear at Mr. Martin, but he had returned to the chair by the window and was turning his brown felt cowboy hat slowly in his hands. Although he was looking firmly toward the floor, she was not foolish enough to believe that he could not hear Anna's soft voice. Jackie couldn't look at either of them. Anna was too brave, and Hank was too gentle. Her heart ached at the forbidden words, while she stared out of the window. She could see the gray overcast morning outside the cramped room and the soft rain beginning to fall. There was no thunder.

"How did you know?" Jackie whispered back. "How long did you know? Why didn't you ever tell me?"

"Why . . . didn't you . . . tell me?" Anna said, her voice warming with a little humor.

"Because—" Jackie fumbled for words. She wanted to explain away her choices as more than cowardice, as rational and right. "I was afraid," she finally finished.

"I know," Anna smiled again. "Me too." Then, as a small coughing fit overtook her, Jackie held Anna's bony hand and listened to the beeps filling the small room increase in frequency and pitch. As her breathing calmed behind the oxygen mask, and her eyes opened again, this time far more tired, she managed her last words for the morning. "Welcome . . . home."

Mr. Martin and Jackie sat together the rest of the morning wordlessly.

Each jagged beep made Jackie wonder when the nurses and doctors would flood the room in an earnest panic, shouting out life-saving orders. Surely this noise meant something serious. The time ticked on, and the nurses came around, it seemed, only at the hour. Jackie did not see a doctor at all that first day.

Hospital time is slow time. The clock on the wall kept slowing down each time Jackie looked at it. She was uncertain whether this was for the best or not. Each slow moment was precious, as she leaned uncomfortably against the wall, with Anna's small hand in hers. Anna, for her part, was in and out of consciousness, and was more or less present when awake. Jackie learned that one of

Anna's pain medications made her more startlingly delirious than at other times. After a nurse upended a syringe of the substance into Anna's IV tubing, Anna's face seemed to melt into the pillow, and then, moments later, she awoke struggling as best she could, yowling like a cat for "Mama!" The machines began their rapid beeping, and the room itself seemed to panic.

Jackie had to leave the room when Mr. Martin explained to Anna again that her mother had already gone to be with Jesus. By this time, the sun had already set.

"You know," Hank Martin said, making Jackie jump when she felt his hand on her shoulder, "you don't have to go back."

"I know; I'll be back tomorrow."

"I mean, you don't have to go back to the city tonight. Your folks live pretty close—"

"I don't think so," Jackie snapped.

"Now listen," Hank Martin said, his voice suddenly turning to gravel, "your folks are good people."

"Mr. Martin—"

"Mr. Martin nothing," he continued. "You're old enough, it's Hank. And I'm telling you that you've got places to stay here now that you're home. Robert has already told you that you can stay out to his place, if you want to."

"Hank," Jackie said, more gently this time. "I could call Bobcat, I suppose."

"That's more like it." Hank's voice softened. "But it's late tonight. Robert's kids are probably asleep. Why don't you just come on over to our place? You remember, we live out off of Rattlesnake Road?"

"I remember," Jackie said, very quietly this time. She started to ask if he had an extra key for her to take, and then realized she wouldn't need to. The Martin door had likely never been locked.

"Good. Just turn off of the county road, the one that passes by the junior high. We're the third driveway on the left, half a mile past where the old Mosby barn used to be up Rattlesnake. If you hit the pond, you've gone too far."

Jackie smiled at the directions. She knew exactly where Hank was indicating, even though the Mosby barn had burned down before she was born, and the junior high had long since merged with another school in the county, leaving the older building abandoned. There were plans, she had learned from Bobcat, to turn it into a flea market. "With the traffic down to the Lake," Bobcat had told her enthusiastically, "it's bound to get plenty of those rich people from Kansas."

"Don't worry about Georgia, either," Hank finished. "She'll growl at you, but she's on a chain, and if she got off it, she'd probably lick you to death anyway."

Jackie's little Nissan four door did not have the optimal suspension to cope with country driving, and her teeth had been rattling since she turned off of the no-account state road's smooth blacktop onto the cracked county road and then onto gravel. But she was quite certain that the county road—now given a four-digit number to name it—had not been paved when she had last driven it, probably fourteen years ago. She watched each mailbox flash its red reflectors at her, and each time her heart jumped as she wondered if it was the gleam of a deer's eye. As her high beams passed over each mailbox, she saw that there were now numbers on them. She had learned that the state now mandated "911 addresses"—numbers which could guide emergency vehicles, instead of the rural route numbers that had indicated addresses in her youth. And yet when asked, neither Bobcat nor Hank had been able to remember their "new" addresses.

So she counted driveways, crawling along in her car, and stopped at the turn-in for the Martin place, and got out in the shivering night to open the gate and to close it after driving through. As she got back into her car to drive the next several hundred yards up the sloping, rutted driveway, she heard Georgia begin to howl. She knew before she saw that Georgia was a Walker hound, with a gorgeous black and tan saddle across her white body.

The realization that she could still tell a dog by its howl chilled her far more than the night.

When she walked into the Martin home, she found it warm. The living room walls teemed with pictures of the Martin family: Hank, Anna and her brother Jason, and Anna's mother, Teresa (dead for six years, hit by a drunk driver out on the no-account state road). The kitchen had stencils of country geese and blue ribbons, and there were coffee mugs by the sink. She took a mug and started the coffee maker up, putting in some of the Folgers from the can by the window, and wandered a little, waiting for the coffee to drip.

In the living room, in the corner, was an upright piano and a guitar case. She remembered Anna practicing her piano lessons in the music room in elementary school, and tears came again. She knew that Hank had taught Jason to play some guitar, as she and Jason had played in pep band together. Jackie had played electric bass because the acoustic/electric guitar her own father had given her sounded too tinny for the band. Although she knew she shouldn't, she opened the guitar case. There was Hank Martin's precious Epiphone acoustic/electric hollow body. It gleamed and seemed to invite her.

Jackie picked it up out of its case and began to tune it automatically. It was flat on all notes, except the B, and she hummed in concert with it as she tuned it back into pitch. E. A. D. G. B. E. The tones that created so much of her childhood, and now— somewhere back in a city she already felt melting away—so many open mic nights at coffee shops and bookstores. At Her Garden. Those places were foreign here, and she shook away the thought.

E. A. D. G. B. E.

Jackie strummed lightly, then with a bit more certainty.

"From this valley they say you are going . . . " she sang under her breath. "We will miss your bright eyes and sweet smile. For they say you are taking the sunshine that has brightened our pathway a while."

She broke down sobbing, but kept playing the classic tune, stopping only to wipe the tears away with the sleeve of her flannel before they could reach the guitar.

Over the next several days, Jackie experienced a high-school reunion, of sorts, as all the teachers who had worked beside Anna at J. C. Nolan High School came to visit her. Many of them had taught Jackie and Anna themselves. At first, Jackie felt afraid when they would walk into the room. She was afraid to be seen holding Anna's tiny hand, and in her fear, she puffed up. She dared them with her glance to say anything, to use any of *those* words, to even so much as look sideways at them.

None did.

Instead, she experienced a strange sort of kindness, sharing grief with her people. She was invited to talk, reminded to eat, and hugged by the most unexpected people. Her former principal, Rosalee Mosby, had touched her lightly on the shoulder, and asked her sincerely, "You are coming back, right?"

Then her fellow J. C. Nolan graduates had come. She remembered slights and cruelty from so many of them, but now these melted into pity; time had made them all either smaller or kinder than she remembered. Jason, Anna's brother, sold cars now in Nolan, and Jackie's junior-high tormentor, Bradley Simmons, mowed his grass. The glorious homecoming queen, Jennifer Sawyer, was a divorced paralegal. Most had children and were only too happy to pull wallet-sized school pictures out of their purses and billfolds to show to Jackie. When asked if she had children, Jackie always said no, and didn't let go of Anna's hand while she said it. Usually, a wife would nudge a husband and the subject would drop.

After asking Hank's permission, Jackie brought the guitar back to the hospital room and would strum it for Anna whenever she requested—which was usually whenever she was awake, before the pain medication that frightened her so much. Jackie could only strum it very softly for fear of the wrath of the nurses. Only the older charge nurse, Elizabeth, seemed understanding. She took the time to smile at Jackie, even when asking her to "keep it down."

Jackie had dreamed, after that first day, that she would return, and she and Anna would have the conversation they had always wanted to have. They would confess their love and tell each other all of their dreams. They would soon be able to laugh at the tragedy of the closet that had kept them apart for thirteen years. The daydreaming always became tenuous at this point, as she would imagine the giddy laughter when the doctors returned to the tiny hospital room to tell them of a strange miracle cure, and that they now had hope—no, certainty—that Anna would live.

Instead, Anna became more confused, and had to be sedated several times to keep from pulling the IV tubing out of her arm. In the silence as Anna's breathing returned to a soft rhythm, Jackie would pick up the guitar and strum it. E. A. D. G. B. E.

Anna lived another five days, softly passing on a Sunday morning, not far from the moment daylight savings time began. This, Jackie had expected. She had stayed awake with Anna all that night and the night before, surrounded by Hank and Jason, Bobcat and his wife, Sarah, who was Anna's best friend.

The only additional pain had been finding a church to bury Anna out of, after people had seen those last few days of Jackie holding her hand. The kindness Jackie and Anna encountered didn't extend in all directions. Jackie let herself hope for a different outcome, as unfamiliar as that felt. But Nowhere Christian politely declined, which broke Jackie's heart, as it was the church Anna's parents had married in. They tried the Methodist and the Baptist churches, but no one seemed too eager. She watched as Hank suffered through their careful excuses, but stopped them each time with an angry "Enough." So a day later, they decided to hold her service at Zimmersheidt and Sons Funeral Home.

At least there were daffodils at the funeral, because Jackie insisted that they reminded her of sunshine and the return of spring after the thaw.

It was five o'clock on the following Monday, and Jackie Neimeyer walked down Main Street in Nowhere with her head in the air. It was warm, at last, and with the sunshine on her shoulders, she no longer needed her jean jacket. She wondered if she would ever be able to return to the city, and in the wondering, she found her answer.

Center

Nebraska's line coach leaned over
the chain-link fence and hit me

in the pads with his clipboard and said,
We'll sign you after the game, big guy.

A forearm wedged under my chin
next play—the tackle was signing for the Bear,

but they knew I could stop him cold.
Snap after snap, I held. Anything

up the gut I could handle. But Sadie
cut me off and kissed me after the game,

and I told Nebraska *no* and married
two months later. We loaded the bed

of the pickup and hummed back to the town
my parents fled seventeen years before.

Sadie and I had our first son
the first year back in Alabama.

He was born solid as an iron ingot,
so we took him down to Legion Field.

All the boys were big in Birmingham,
but the old tackle breached the line,

and I roared and slapped the bald man's head
in front of me. I wouldn't have let him through.

Sadie cheered again, too, and saw me
holding our son up like a ball.

The next year, Sadie tucked him under
her arm and took the truck to the store. I found it

later, doors open, down a hillside,
Sadie gutted in the snow. I shouted at the woods

but couldn't get the words off. *False
start* in my head. I felt the arm again

against my throat. I heard the sharp whistle
of a warbler. Its breast burned in the pine.

Forecasting

You remember slanted clouds inching their way
      to the parched dust beneath your feet,
            a sufficient warning for welcome.

This foreign, swollen air offers no advent—
      a single electric signature blasts tides
            to flood horizons. Zephyrs tease
      and whisk leaves before whirlwinds surge us
to the basement, wishing we'd pared
      branches fighting the kitchen window.

Yet my core dances when storms baptize
      wisteria's banks and drown my gravel shortcuts,
            just as you don't mind rattles ready
      to strike or coyotes dizzy with drought.
You promise it's all worth a desert christening,
      the Sangre de Christo cresting every deluge.

We know home resides in our threaded frames,
but we are rooted guilty in love
with our own earths, dangers
and distance be damned. We can't deny
these worlds between us. Native as we seem
cloaked together by pilgrim clouds,

where one chest overflows,
the other is a well
pierced with thirst for elsewhere.

The Hawk

A black stamp against braided clouds,
it spiraled our grassy shadows. *Look, look!*
he insisted, as if we'd caught God

dropping us a dark pearl. Maybe we had.
Maybe, he hoped, it would ripple us
and pull my gaze to what arrested his,

eyes meeting again in the middle distance
if nowhere else. Maybe joint witness can redirect
a vision. But I censored wonder, untouched

to shrivel like a peach, skin sliming off by the time
my hunger erupted empty. I'd heard the fullest way
to love was to not. Maybe it isn't.

Later, alone, my neck twisted searching sky
for what I knew had vanished. We both knew
you can only circle a question so long.

Marriage Brooms

We don't keep them by the window, where light
lances through the shades, lining our bookshelves
with the years we've stood together. Instead, we rest
them in the gentler sun, where softened rays silhouette
their caress. They've swept a sacred corner
for themselves, refusing to collect wandering books
or the dog's woolly tumbleweeds.

A friend wove them one lonely Midwestern winter.
His frozen fingers crafted a blessing and learned
the sting of devotion's tender tedium.
They arrived late with apologies for foregoing
the standard wedding gifts—blenders, bedding,
what we call useful. Some treasures aren't
meant for tidying life.

The purest loves always seem eccentric,
unessential. We rarely hunger for what sustains.
Love labors in hope alone that it be welcome
if not cherished, that its grace-twined gifts
might, for a moment, honor this dust.

KATHY M. BATES

Where There's Fire

I SIT AROUND A BONFIRE with close friends one December evening. We pass a bottle of "here try this" around our merry circle—making sure not to get too close to the flames, only near enough to soak up as much of the emanating warmth as possible. I turn my head away from the fire's light, close my eyes, and take a deep frigid breath, winter filling my lungs to capacity. Sometimes I swear I can smell the chill in the air, almost vivid enough to give it a name of its own: fear, danger—*something*. But here, among the safety of my companions, I am blissfully content and safe.

A piece of wood settles, and tension grips the base of my neck. My flinch goes unnoticed, but my pulse's quickening beat is strong enough to remain until I rally the will to push the uneasy feeling to the back of my mind. It isn't the flame itself that makes me anxious. It's the tiny burst of smoke that follows the flicker's edge. It's the ever-so-slight change in scent carried on the wind swirling around our circle, threatening to fuse my bones into place more than the cold temperature if I'm not careful. I am aware that I have to be aware as I remember moments I might not want to remember. The smoky concoction causes a chain reaction of memories seemingly impossible to hold back.

When we recall our past, we often hear what we want to hear and see what we want to see. Limitations exist even if self-imposed. But memories connected to scents are stronger than any other sense memory. Sometimes I step away from the fire, avoiding the puffs of smoke as they dissipate. Other times I stand close and let the

53

odors, thick and rich, sweet and bitter, soak into my clothes and skin. Because I can step toward the fire and smoke, I know I have almost healed, but regardless, a hint of danger remains etched in memory, carved into bone and imprinted on cells.

* * *

In June of 1981, my family of four lived in Augusta, Georgia, just a few miles from my grandparents' house. Eight days after my fifth birthday, a fire broke out in the basement stairwell just outside our apartment door. I learned from newspaper clippings that it must have started a little after six o'clock in the morning, the firetrucks allegedly responding by 6:16. I couldn't have known what time it was myself, too disoriented and blinded by smoke-filled rooms.

Our apartment on the basement level was long and narrow. It was a tiny home but big enough for an efficiency kitchen, a small living room area, two bedrooms, and one shared bathroom. There was a small, long window running across half the living room, the top edge almost touching the corner of the low ceiling. One identical but shorter window was in each of the bedrooms, all at ground level on the side of the building. If I stood on my tiptoes and backed away from the wall, I could see the dirt and grass on the other side of the glass pane.

I remember not sleeping well the night before.

I remember being the first to smell the smoke.

I remember nearly everything.

* * *

I read a study once that said smells and emotion are stored as one memory, and in our earliest years, when we experience odors for the first time, we attach meaning to what we will like and hate for the rest of our lives. I'm not sure about liking or hating something for the rest of my life; I tend to believe that we can decide to change our opinions at any time, much like adapting for survival. But I am sure about the memory part—how I have tied odors and fragrances to an emotional response. It's basic brain science. Senses have to detour like a relay station through the thalamus before heading to various areas of the brain, but smells go straight to the source related to emotion and memory—an evocative power—and mine saved me.

* * *

I must have sensed the faint odor during its initial, slow burn. It was sweet, almost syrupy. That part of the city had an abundance of pine trees; it might have been that. Or maybe dust, like a heater when you turn it on for the first time after the temperatures start to drop, but it was June. If I had been older, I might have said my notions of smell were romanticized, and it was more of a synthetic odor than anything else.

Rubbing my eyes, I walked into my parents' room and tried to wake my mom. It wasn't unusual for me. She would pat my arm and tell me to go back to bed. That morning was no different. I reluctantly walked back to the hallway and stood in the doorway of my room I shared with my sister. She was still sound asleep inside, and I almost went in, but I just stood there like I was waiting to piece together the rest of a puzzle. Something wasn't quite right, as if my mom had left the stove on. But it wasn't, and the previous night's taco mess had been cleaned, and the trash bagged.

I stepped into the living room and moved a few feet closer to the front door, where the scent was stronger—sweet and dusty. The seal around the front door wasn't the best. It was thin, and on most days, sounds echoed through the stairwell, people moving around, fighting or crying. That morning, I didn't hear anything but saw smoke pushing forcefully through the gaps around the door like cracks had tripled in size.

Describing panic is much like describing the most exciting carnival ride imaginable, minus the good. By age five, I hadn't been to a carnival or fair that I could remember, but now I know the thrill of the rides, the way my stomach clenches in nervous anticipation on the rickety uphill climb of a wooden gem-of-a coaster, the pitch-point pause at the top before the fall that releases all the energy into a perfect, good scream of excitement. But trying to relay my emotions as my bare feet tore across the carpet, down the hall, running back into their room screaming at the top of my lungs—all the good was gone.

As I stood on my mom's side of the bed screaming, they still didn't know what was happening. They hadn't seen anything or smelled anything, but when they did, I saw it in their eyes, their panic rising to meet my own. Then something popped in the stairwell loud enough to echo through the apartment, like someone throwing a thick-bottomed drinking glass against the apartment door. They both raced into action. Mom grabbed my arm tight enough to constrict blood flow and yelled for my sister to get up. In the living room, we stood back as my dad reached to the ceiling and broke out the windows running parallel to the ground. Mom escaped first so she could help pull us out. My sister followed.

When it was my turn, my dad raised his arms and pushed me up and over the edge of the window frame toward one of the firefighter's outstretched arms. My legs hadn't cleared, but he continued to push. On the other side, I grabbed at handfuls of dead grass and dirt until a stranger wrapped his hands around my chest and pulled. Another responder must have been standing by to help my dad, but I was already being carried away.

I was set on the hood of a stranger's broken-down car, and someone wrapped a blanket around my shoulders just like in the movies. But what the movies don't always show is the separation. My mom and sister had been ushered to the other side of the parking lot, far enough away to be on the opposite side of another firetruck that had just arrived. My dad was still coming out of our apartment's tiny windows, and I was sitting alone. I'm sure it was only for a few seconds, but it seemed like a lifetime in my memory.

Black and gray smoke caught in a gust of wind. I sucked it in by mistake and coughed roughly, to the point of gagging. I had been around cigarette smoke before. My WWII-veteran grandpa spent most of his day sitting around the kitchen table chain smoking cigars or cigarettes while staring at, not reading, a newspaper. Unsmoked, the rolled tobacco was almost sweet, but fire and smoke morphed it into something I could never bring myself to appreciate as others might. The smoke inside the building was nothing like the tolerable smoke from around the kitchen table, burning dry holes in my throat instead. I knew I needed to move, to get to my mom.

I wiped my nose as clean as I could with a corner of the blanket, enough to smear the ash and dirt around my nose. The southern summer heat was rising, and it radiated off the car's hood even in the early morning hours. The backs of my legs were sticky with humidity as I slid from the hood until my bare feet touched the warm ground.

"Child, you're bleeding," a neighbor said, pointing to the front side of my lower leg. I looked down, eyes wide. A deep, thick, dark red line marked a nearly straight path starting at my ankle and extending up to just below my kneecap. The gash must have been stable to a point, held together by adrenaline and confusion, but now, shifting under the pressure of my movements, it began to gush in torrents down and around the surrounding skin, trailing the ground.

I didn't recall a tone of fear in her voice, especially at that moment, even though fear was my entire world. She didn't seem panicked either, even though my morning had been encapsulated by it.

"Hurry, bring her inside."

At first, my feet were on the ground, wet and warm with hose water, then I floated. Most of my senses began to dwindle to flashing sensations, but the smell still had strength. It lingered, following on clouds around me. Someone carried me into an apartment across the parking lot. Smoky odors seemed to disperse but not die at first as they blended with new ones, merged with others: her, the man carrying me, everything foreign but familiar. Aftershave and cigarette smoke pressed against my cheek, replaced by coffee, warm biscuits, and bath wash. Nothing was as strong as the smoke had been outside—all I knew was that it was better.

"Mind the faucet and watch the blood," the woman said. I was half awake and half asleep, inside a weird in-between dream world that seemed to be unable to make up its mind. Did it want to be painful? Comforting? She was somebody's mom, somebody's grandma. I caught glimpses of eye-level pictures in the rooms on the way to her bathroom, surrounding me with a warmth that smelled like a home of blessing and love.

The man wrapped part of the blanket under my dangling legs and feet like a bowl. He put me down on the edge of the bathtub, and they turned the water on, washing away the blood streaming down my leg. They were talking, but only a little made it through the fog settling over me.

"They on their way," I heard him say as they switched places. The woman wrapped my leg in a clean towel and another around my body. Her laundry detergent must have been the same kind *my* grandma used. Did I tell her that? Did I say anything while my body weakened, letting go of all these new smells and sensations?

"She gon' be alright," she said moments before I lost consciousness.

I knew I would be.

I remember waking up in the hospital, where antiseptic replaced the smoky coating on the insides of my lungs. Eighteen stitches seemed to take forever to heal, even though it was closer to two or three months. Then it took years more to ease the negative emotions that arose every time I saw a building in flames, even longer if billowing black smoke clouded the area. It took more than twenty years to attach the words "trauma response," giving a name to something that seemed illogical while making perfect sense.

I wouldn't say I'm afraid of fire, more that I'm captivated by it. I am fascinated that a visual effect can conjure polarized emotions. The happiness of a fire warming a hearth during the holidays, the excitement of a bonfire on the beach, or fear—as flames destroy a building where people might be trapped inside. A force strong enough to burn forests and cities.

And then there's smoke—the remains.

That morning years ago, I knew the presence of fire but never saw the flames that destroyed the three levels of our apartment's stairwell and damaged presumably safe homes. I never once saw the intruder who burst through the entrance and crept up and along the front of the building, charring the brick and wood and paint. I never saw the flames—only the smoke. In my mind, I can still remember the smells more than anything, those that forced memories to implant and associate in vivid detail.

* * *

We moved a lot back then, all over the South, from Georgia to Texas, everywhere in between and back again. Eventually, I recognized that the air smells a little different in each home within a home. Sometimes it's subtle and comforting, like a breeze catching the tang of a local barbeque joint. Then sometimes pungent, standing downwind to a paper mill. Smoke adds a variant all its own, concocting new mixtures ready to ride the wind but still just a little different each place—each time.

Now I sit with my friends outside, around a blazing fire, my legs covered in layers staving off an early winter breeze. There's still a scar underneath, one side that aches when the weather changes. But that's just a physical mark. The trauma responses are less predictable and often, thankfully, less visual. I've learned to love to watch a roaring fire in an open fireplace—but never too close in case the smoke lingers, threatening to twist a heavy knot in my stomach. I've learned to adapt, but sometimes I still wake up in the middle of the night wondering if something is burning. Then when fall rolls around, and people light their furnaces and host their bonfires, I inhale deeply, letting the chilled air fill my lungs, and I remember being five years old.

I remember not sleeping well the night before.

I remember being the first to smell the smoke.

I remember nearly everything.

The Audible Waters of Meribah

Timer Number 4: The fire brigade takes in Gengen Where, who has become hard of hearing.

Read me as a
traveling group. Hard to imagine one
goes to bed dry

while another
goes deaf, quenched. In a future with no sound
the only perfection is

discernible
wind through unburnt leg hairs.
From the top of Engine One

we are drafting
from two folding water tanks.
If I turn my head this way

what I can hear
is the gush of water
from Tanker Two

dumping warm brown
pond water.
(What old woman is fishing

in a duck pond
two hundred acres from here
knowing she's afloat in

someone's savior?)
This way and I can only hear
the unbroken cheeky growl

of all our trucks.

Join me patting
low down the hallway one night soon,
scraping the floor with an ax handle.

One foot hooked to
the door jamb behind us.
The floor will be spotted with

pill-sized hearing
aid batteries. Our senses spread flat through crisping halls,
all of us unready for the grass

fire up the road
the week after next.

Hanging the Bat House

I.

I can see down into what used to be
a cattle dipping pond,
where at least one horse is buried
and lawnmower batteries rot.
I can hear geese. I can smell rooftops.

II.

White knuckling the swaying
branchless pine,
twenty-five feet high, this is also where I keep
my fog knife safe. Folded up
in the airstream. It rains. It is raining.

III.

Great puddles of thinking just deep enough
to please the bright Indian Runner
and the weight of some fat Muscovy. Water
seeks gaps in suet. To ruin the bird's seed.
To keep me in bed. To yawn all over me.

IV.

I begin churning clarity
the moment I hear thunder on the way,
bouncing over the surface
of the forest's ready ministries. They have settled
and spread out as a fog at twenty-five feet above the valley floor.

V.

It still rumbles. Now the thickness
of dawn and its sister,
an overfed cat, join me
at the top of the swaying naked pine.
We sway. We are swaying.

VI.

We never know where to go with this
moment. We never know where to go with
this top-heavy moment. Like three
sedate Harold Lloyds.
Accidentally going on with things. Slicing nothing.

CASEY SPINKS

Carter's Walk

I carried you, naked except for a diaper,
to the woods and back,
and I spoke to you words
about the winter season,
its gray and brown colors and their reasons,
of the bare trees and expectancy of spring;
one day you'd understand;
we walked to a grove,
and I showed you the trunks of trees specific—
this one pine, that one oak—
and I took your hand
to touch the bark, but you recoiled—
it's alright: unmoving things are frightening,
and that never changes;
then changing arms, I carried you back slowly
to the house you'll be raised in—
in that sense, holy—
and I spoke some more of little things
and one day you'll speak to answer;
but today, your curious eyes, ranging looks,

soft blond hair swaying
in the stillness
on Christmas day under the wooded canopy:
all of it was enough,
an uncle's delight,
and perhaps it shall have helped you sleep well tonight
—it will give rest to me.

Fragile Objects

WHEN BUB'S FATHER picked him up from school in the new silver commuter car with the sunroof, he said they were going to drive over to the boy's grandmother's house in the next county. They would help her out. Maybe they would make her dinner. It should be fun, Dad said. Bub answered only by puckering his face. He threw his backpack onto the soft gray upholstery of the back seat, flung his body limply after it, and buckled up.

Bub and his mother and father lived in the city, but his grandmother, Dad's mother, lived in a small house across the bay, one county over. The long drive out of the city, past the tall robot-shaped government buildings and the one office tower, then through the tunnel and across the water, might have left the boy feeling lost if he had not known this route ever since he was tall enough to sit up and see through the back window of a car.

Mardi Gras had long since ended, but strings of purple and gold beads still clung to the branches of the oaks. The spring had drawn on until it was no longer the lime-and-magenta fireworks show of late February and early March but the humid summerlike sunbath of late April. As they drove across the water along the causeway, a low road that threaded under a long bridge that crossed it yet came to the same destination, Bub heard his father explaining the situation to him—*these prescriptions make her tired, the loneliness makes her sad; she needs better nutrition, more companionship.*

The long words meant no more to the boy than the names of cars or of the parts of the long bridge, which he could see both displayed through the car window and reflected in the glare on the inner surface of it. The words, like the images, rolled past him without making any significant contact.

Bub felt a frustration like an eyelash in the eye. The feeling seemed to be located inside the double images on the curved glass of the car window. He could look at the Bayway rising out of the choppy brown water on its pilings but could never hold in his hands the winches and wrenches needed to tighten the bolts, the levers of the amphibious machinery used to set the long supports in place. He could ride only in the back seat of the lacquered silver car, never the front seat, much less put his hands on the wheel.

Not that he much wanted the responsibility of driving. Bub had seen a car crash on the highway once, where a single lane in each direction wove through what used to be plantation land but was now mostly subdivisions and horse farms. That day he and his mother and father had been returning from some megachurch event, some revivalist meeting that had intrigued his mother's mind, in a big-roofed rural arena connected to the fairgrounds of the next state over.

The boy could not have told what they had gained by going to the revival. All he remembered of the event was the pink stage lights, the loud singing, and the hot humidity, the overheated fog around him created by flabby adult bodies swaying and crying. But he could have told in detail, if Dad had thought to ask him, about the body on the gurney at the roadside afterward, already draped in a white sheet.

Bub's mother had shrieked and twisted around to the back, stretching her hand wildly toward his eyes—he was an only child—"Don't look, don't look!"—but he had seen: the green, green grass, the orange clay, the white sheet, like the Irish flag displayed in school on International Day last year. Then he had been in second grade, still practically a baby. He hadn't even known what death meant before, that it meant you really went away from your body and you never came back into it. That was how much no one wanted to teach him real things.

At the end of the long causeway the car's engine hummed lower, growling as it pulled up the highway ramp, past the old Civil War fort crowning the hill, through the clear-cut area past the new strip malls and the Zaxby's and Chick-Fil-A chicken restaurants, and then into the woods. Dad drove past the newer subdivisions, stopped at the double-bulbed caution signal blinking yellow, and took a turn away from the main road toward the older parts of the little town. Bub noted each landmark: the post office and the public school, four or five different churches, the gas station, the shrimp restaurant. Next they passed the place with the courtyard fenced in by weathered boards, umbrella tables, banana trees, and year-round Christmas lights, the place that Dad had said was bad. Fishing nets, dirty ones, were strung across the front entry and along the fence. Bub had once asked why these were put here and had been told the nets were for trapping souls. He had not asked any more questions after that. He had not stopped having questions; he had just stopped asking them. Adult talk of souls seemed to be meant to put a stop to children's questions, either by spreading wishful vagueness or inducing deliberate terror. Bub received this as the way things were and, therefore, as the way they ought to be.

The silver coupe wove its way down another two-lane road through woods before it pulled to a stop in the driveway of Bub's grandmother's place, a barn-red wooden shotgun house with a screened-in porch and a black iron star in a circle hung on the front outer wall. At the very end of the level asphalt drive, in line with the deck and the little jetty that led out over the deep creek behind the house, there sat parked an ancient light-blue Cadillac, its wheel wells traced with rust.

Bub and his father climbed out of the low coupe and entered

the porch. The screen door, with its familiar sleeve-snagging rip in the wire mesh, rattled on its hinges when they passed through it. Bub's muscles clenched up as if this tension could hold his clothes away from the teeth of the tear.

Inside the house held an atmosphere of sleep and long hours where waking did not mean much. The cool air smelled of musty vinyl, Ivory soap, potpourri, and cooking grease. Right now, above the smells of cleansing and decay, there was overlaid an odor of sour coffee left on the hot plate to burn.

Grandma had stacked and shelved her belongings all over the main room in soft and delicate profusion. The couches, baby-pink velour, suffocated under multiple zigzag and granny-square afghans in wildly discordant colors: mustard, cranberry, rust, aquamarine.

The coffee tables, glass-topped wood, and the cabinets along the walls held curiosities Bub knew he must never touch: A spun-glass swan, under a willow tree whose branches were also made of thin filaments of glass, rested on a mirror that represented a pool of clear water. The swan's reflection under the willow looked just like another swan swimming beneath, upside down. Two tiny glass cygnets swam after it, mirrored like the mother; Bub had been spanked as a toddler for pocketing one. An apothecary jar of colored marbles likewise made Bub's fingers itch. Bronze baby shoes, as if just dropped from little feet, rested beside plaster hands that seemed to pray. Demitasse cups yearned open next to porcelain roses that fooled you into thinking they bloomed. Sprays of dried cotton bolls bristled from crystal bud vases. Against one wall stood a crazed grandfather clock that struck the quarter hour with a jangle every thirteen minutes.

The clock occupied the spot that, in most houses, would be filled by a television. Here there was an old cabinet set, which Dad had said was from the 1950s and which still used wire rabbit-ears on top and glass tubes inside, but the set had not worked for as long as Bub could remember. The walls were lined with old hardback books, some in jackets, others in woven cloth covers, which he had never seen anyone take down to read.

This place Bub both loved and hated. It meant for him an enclosed world, an olden-times world, above all a female world that would never welcome him or belong to him and toward which he felt at the same time drawn and disgusted. Whenever he remembered that he belonged to the blessed brotherhood of those who ran faster and threw harder and could not ever, ever grow up to be helpless mothers with helpless babies or grandmothers stuck in stuffy old houses, the knowledge made him want to jump and dance.

"Mom?" Bub's father called. With his thick, heavy tread he stepped over the threshold into the living room. The floorboards shivered; the threads of the glass willow branches rattled. Bub walked after his father, taking pleasure in the lightness of his own step.

In the daffodil-colored kitchen they found Grandma seated at the round table, in a wooden chair. On the waxy table cover in front of her there rested a cup of warm milky coffee. Beside it a little box with seven doors sat, half the doors open. The veiny hands held the warm cup but didn't lift it to the loose mouth, which, when Grandma looked in Bub's father's direction, turned from slack sorrow to a rictus of delight.

"Daniel," said the old woman.

"Mom," Dad said. He looked not at her but, as he kissed her cotton-soft and lightly fuzzy forehead, at the pill box on the table.

"What did you do? It's only Tuesday."

"Well, yesterday was Tuesday. Today cain't be Tuesday too," she said in a tone of voice Bub knew well. It was the same tone his own mother took whenever he wanted to wear beach sandals on a rainy day or a fleece jacket in August.

"You take you a look right here at this calendar," Grandma went on. From the lazy Susan in the middle of the table she produced a much-folded booklet.

"Mom, this calendar is from last year." Bub's father inspected the plastic doors of the box again. "You say you took these yesterday?" he asked, placing his finger on the first box marked T.

"And these today." She nodded and pointed to the W.

Dad checked the M box and found it still full of little tablets. His relief was visible on his face. "Well, we can straighten it all out by Saturday," he said. He gave the grandmother a little sidewise hug and then, breathing in, reached down to lift her coffee cup to his face.

"Mom, this milk is off. Don't drink any more of it." He stepped to the sink and poured the contents of the cup down the disposal. Then he went to the fridge to check for the rest of the carton.

Bub sat statue-still through all this business. He had a role in this many-times-replayed scene, and he knew it very well. Until he heard his cue, he sat with his feet tucked under him in a kitchen chair. Bub would be scolded if he swung his legs, if he attempted to rise, if he yawned or made a face, if he bit his nails or lips, if he picked his nose or scratched his skin anywhere it itched, if he touched anything that looked interesting. In a minute he would be asked a question to which he was expected to answer Yes Ma'am and Thank You. Until then he sat studying the clementine paisley pattern of the tablecloth and debating within himself whether tracing the teardrops with a fingertip might invite reproof.

"Godwin," warbled the grandmother. The boy suppressed a wince. Not only at school, but in front of other children at all times, he always gave his name as Bub. The self-adopted nickname meant nothing to him; that was why he liked it.

"Godwin," she repeated, while he was still collecting his thoughts.

"Yes ma'am," Bub said.

"Go in the pantry door there, would you, and bring me the blue tin with the snowflake lid. If we have any cookies today, would you like one?"

"Yes ma'am. Thank you."

There were always cookies. They were usually stale. Bub would be given one, not seven or four or two, no matter how small they were or how hungry he was. About all of this he had learned by long practice not to argue.

Today the tin brought luck: gingerbread windmills studded with almonds. The cookies were hard but not too much so. His father must have brought groceries over the weekend, although Bub was sure he didn't know when, because his parents hadn't fought, and a fight between his parents usually preceded or followed any trip to his grandmother's.

Bub made his windmill last while his father washed dishes, drained the spoiled milk down the disposal, rinsed the carton, scrubbed the sink, peeled carrots, cut open a plastic pouch of meat, and finally shoved meat and carrots off their flat board and into a lidded pot that plugged into the wall. Dad poured water into the pot and shook in salt and pepper before securing the lid on top and then pressing some buttons. Bub's grandmother also watched this process while mouthing a windmill cookie. Finally Dad microwaved a cup of water and brought it to the table with a weedy-smelling tea bag inside of it. He put the cup on the table where Grandma's coffee had been before, next to the row of damp almond slivers she had first removed from her cookie with her gums and then removed from her mouth with her fingers, laying each ivory nut down one by one on a paper napkin atop the plastic-coated cloth.

"Careful, it's hot," Dad said of the tea. "Let it steep."

The three sat staring at each other across the table for a moment or two. Bub ran scenarios in his mind for what could happen next, based on past visits. The rotary phone on the wall could shrill its firehouse ring, and his mother could be on the other end, demanding audibly to know why the hell her husband wasn't home yet, why he wasn't picking up his cell either. His grandmother could spill her scalding tea, resulting in another trip to urgent care that would end in another talking-to from another tired-looking nurse in scrubs printed with pink and purple flowers. Bub knew his father did not take such women—women like the nurse, or like Bub's own mother—seriously. None of them compared to Grandma favorably: "No experience of life," he would say afterward. "No toughness of character. Never had to pull themselves up in the world. Entitled. Then they dress up in white coats and try to tell you what's what. Wonder how they'd hold up if they had had to make biscuits for another family's children at five every morning from the time they were seven years old, and scrub the floors when the others were all learning to write and to figure, and not be allowed to sleep till the laundry was all clean and folded." Early in her life the grandmother's adoptive family had made a Cinderella of her, a Cinderella before the dress and the ball. None of her connections, from the grandfather who had played the role of prince to the boy at the end of the family line, had ever been allowed to forget this.

Anything could happen now, Bub thought. An airplane could land on the house. An alligator could crawl through the plate-glass sliding door of the back porch. But probably it wouldn't. What would probably happen was this. The three of them would move with slow steps to the living room. Dad would help Grandma to a seat on the couch. They would sit and sit. They might talk or not. The grandfather clock would chime, out of tune and time. After the fourth chime they would be allowed to leave. And as they pulled out of the vine-canopied drive Bub would sigh with guilty relief. He would again have spent an hour staring through the never-opened back door at the creek: slow work, no story, but while it went forward, not so bad or so boring. The creek rippled green and brown. Bub could see dragonflies running their switchback plays over it, hear the rhythmic hip-hop songs of frogs. Once he had seen a frog eat a whole dragonfly right near the window on a garden flagstone. That had been worth the hypnosis of the foregoing thirty-eight minutes. The wings had stuck out of the squashy beak so crazily. In the low silver gloom of the cloud-screened sun off the water, each cell had glistened.

Now as Bub had predicted, the three generations moved to the living room, where Bub and Dad—"so good to see my menfolk," Grandma said—sat on the stiff pink cushions. Dad helped Grandma into her own recliner, a forest green overstuffed chair draped with a worn, nubby cream afghan, before coming to sit on the couch with his elbows on his knees. His torso canted forward like the boom of an excavator.

"Time we got you to the dentist soon, Mom, seems like," Dad said after a moment.

"Oh Danny, it ain't worth the trouble. Ain't got many teeth left worth a damn nor many more months left to put up with 'em."

This was, as far as Bub could remember, the exact same line his grandmother had been repeating to his father for years and years, and not only about teeth.

"And the eye doctor?"

"Ain't no point."

"High time I got the oil changed in your car, though," Dad said in a flat voice.

"Oh no you don't," Grandma warbled. "That's how you get my keys. Then I don't ever drive again. I know all the tricks, you see. How I know is I go to church. All those ladies know every back way to get things done. Make happen what they want, stop what they don't. Oh you bet they do. I ain't giving up no keys, not me. You'll have to find some better trick than that."

"Mom, it's no trick. That car sits in the driveway twenty days outta twenty-one. Least we can do's to keep it maintained for ya."

"Oh I know who 'we' are too. That wife put you up to this. You tell her I know she did and you tell me what she says back to that too."

"Mama, there's no trick," Dad repeated quietly.

"Oh I know what there is and what there ain't. I know enough. By now I heard enough too."

"I can get the keys from where you keep them if I want to. But I'd rather have you give them to me."

"Huh. Mighta been born at night but it warn't last night." The windmill sweetness and peace had all gone from her face. Her features had drawn tight shut like the petals of an insulted morning glory.

"Well, if it has to be like that—"

"Oh don't mind me, I'm just a stupid old woman."

A terrible silence fell. Into it the clock jangled.

"I saw Betty the other day down to the store," Dad spoke, into more silence. Betty was the wife of the pastor at the grandmother's church. Grandma did not like Betty but loved to hear of her minor transgressions. Now she refused even this obvious peace offering. Bub pushed the dull edge of his school shoe sole very cautiously down the line of charcoal grout between two dirty white tiles on the floor.

"Winny here got ninety-seven on his last math quiz," Dad tried again. No response.

"Next month we're going up to the fish camp on Wheeler Lake," he then told the silence. "Last time Winny caught a catfish bigger 'n—"

Dad's upheld hands took the shape of a goalpost, between which the full tea mug flew like a football. The liquid fanned out all along the floor, a slick splatter on the tiles. The cup split in two against the drywall behind the couch: Bub read the inscription #1 *Grandma* split into syllables with eerie, wrong perfection.

"Shut up talkin' to me like that," Grandma snapped. "I got more where that come from."

"Your backwoods comes out when you're angry," Dad muttered under his breath.

"What was that?"

"Nothin'. Go get a towel, Win."

Quickly Bub rose and stepped around the spill, toward the front closet where, in an old laundry hamper, large and small cleaning rags were kept.

"And the mop," his father called after him.

While Bub was busy in the front hall, Dad, stumping along in his son's wake, murmured several rapid sentences in a low rumble the boy strained to hear. Bub couldn't, however, make any words out. Finally, realizing that his quiet and stillness must by now seem to mean mischief, Bub loaded up mop and rags in a red bucket that stood close and turned to hand the bundle to his father. He had never seen such a look on the man's face.

"Well if that's how it is," his father was repeating. "If that's—"

Dad cut his own words short then. He took the mop from his son and began to push the puddle of chamomile around on the tile with the splayed, ropy strings.

Bub stood watching by the front door, very still as if in a deer blind, as if the safest thing to do might be to shrink and calcify, to become one of the knick-knacks on the shelves and credenzas. If he called no attention to himself at all, this might stop happening, or turn out never to have really started.

"Win, go get in the car."

Dad turned and tossed him the keys to the silver coupe. They hit Bub in the shin and clattered to the tile, where he crouched with infinitesimal slowness to pick them up.

"Win! Now," his father boomed. A flash of lightning sheared a branch off an oak and sent it crashing into a chain link fence: no it didn't, the sun remained stubbornly out, and Bub realized the sound had been the scream of the hinges in his grandmother's recliner as she pushed in the footrest and rose to point her accusing finger at his father.

"You! Done hurt me all your life," she cried. "Hurt me comin' out. Hurt me failin' school. Hurt me makin' eyes and makin' chirrun with that little piece of sumpin'. Hurt me makin' plans about me I ain't never agreed to. Well I ain't never agreed. I ain't never agreed to any of it. They cain't tell me it's in the vows. I said love honor and obey. Obey *him*. Not *you*."

Son and father stood like statues. They calcified, shrank. Yes, the safest thing to be, in that room at any given moment, would have been a piece of porcelain. You would have been put behind glass and protected. Cherished.

"Win. Go."

There was a plea in it now. Bub picked up the keys and went.

Out in the car he stared around the yard and driveway. A box garden held sprouts of spinach and lettuce. When he was smaller he had helped to plant seeds here. Later in the summer there would be tomato vines, yellow squash, long green zucchini. When had his grandmother found the strength to dig the soil and weed the beds? It couldn't have been her doing. She could barely walk from her table to her chair without help. It must have been his father. His father who was always telling his mother there was no time, no money, for the deck or the flowers or the vegetables in their own backyard. So why—? Because their house was not at the center. It would never be at the center. For his father, this was the center.

The screen door opened. Dad ran out holding a second set of keys in his hands and, with too much force, grabbed the handle of the driver's door and threw it open. The car's small frame trembled. Dad threw the new set of keys into Bub's lap.

"Hold those," Dad said. He started the silver car and laid his foot on the brake. Then he took out his phone and began texting.

His eyes remained focused on the screen while Bub watched the torn screen door shudder open a second time.

"Dad?" said Bub.

"Not now," Dad answered.

"Just . . . it's . . . "

"I said not now."

Once at a sleepover with classmates Bub had secretly watched a horror movie that had a girl monster in it. The story had been that the girl had died, drowned in a well, but because of some ancient curse she couldn't stay in the well but instead was forced to come out and attack people who watched the horror movie and now here she came, robed in white, crouched over, hair covering her face, until you saw—

Bub's grandmother had made her way toward the car at the same incremental speed, in the same hunched and scuttling way, as the girl-monster in the movie. She tapped the glass of the passenger window. Bub's heart raced.

"Dad!'" he shrieked.

"Son."

Bub saw his father's rage on one side, his grandmother's on the other, and didn't know which he feared more.

"Roll down the window," Dad told him.

As soon as the glass came open a half inch the old woman's twisted fingers pushed through the crack. Something fell with a plink to land, again, in Bub's lap. Bub picked the object up: two brass keys on a strong silver loop with a green plastic numeral 1 hooked onto it.

"Grandma, your house keys . . . "

"Won't need them no more."

"Mom! Mama—"

"Cain't go nowhere, don't need to lock up after. Ain't leavin' here again so what does it matter. Next y'all gon come up in here, tag all my things. You want this and he wants that. Who's gon take care of it all like I done? Y'all with them empty houses y'all never set foot in more time'n it takes to eat and piss and sleep? Y'all want my wedding china, my chifforobes, my collectibles? What for, for chamber pots? Who's it all gon matter to? You boy? Godwin! you gon take care a my things for me? You gon dust the swans and the willow with a feather? You gon leave the roses bloom all year? Naw. You gon break 'em is what you gon do. With a baseball bat. Soon's I'm cold if not before."

"Mom. This is enough in front of—"

"You don't tell me what's enough. After all I done. All I hurt."

His father's face seemed to have melted. "Don't talk like that. When I owe you so m—mm—"

"Shut up that cryin'. You don't owe me nothin'."

The grandmother began her slow hitch and shuffle back to the house. Bub's father jolted out of the car and followed her as fast as he could, hoisting his extra weight along. When he touched her elbow to support her, the cane fell from her hand, and she folded to the ground like something made of origami paper.

When Bub's own mother asked him about it much later, Bub would not be able to remember certain parts of what happened next. Not for years would he recall the sound his grandmother's bones made against the asphalt, the sound that came from his father's throat when he heard it. It would not make sense to him, either, the place where the two of them had come to rest at the head of the drive, near the Cadillac, instead of on the front step where they ought to have been. Bub only knew at the time that his father had left the car running with him inside it. Bub had been told that, in this case, he must not move or unbuckle his seat belt until an adult came to turn the car off. Yet he knew that whatever else had happened, it was bad. His father might really need help. Bub saw he would have to figure this one out alone.

One time, Bub's mother had taught him how to climb across the console and into the driver's seat to turn off the ignition. This was what Bub had been trying to do to the silver coupe, but the key in the ignition wouldn't turn; it only made a skirling locust noise. So Bub looked where his mother had told him to look and, sure enough, the car had been left in Neutral, not Park.

So Bub grabbed the lever, also like he had been shown, and pushed up with all his might, but not far enough. The lever snapped, not from N to P, but from N to R. From the direction of the back axle he felt a lurch. Bub shouted through the closed window for his father's help as he pushed the lever harder than ever and kicked out with his foot while at the same time he tried with both thumbs to press in the button as he pushed: go up to P, up to P, P for park, *P for protect, P for pulverize-me-not. Go go go why won't the thing go? What did I do before?*, Bub asked himself, even as his kicking foot came in contact with the wrong pedal, not the brake but the accelerator, and the car roared into motion, shooting backward across both empty lanes of the road before thundering to rest against a young tree in a ditch full of red sumac, Virginia creeper, and immature live oaks and pines. On impact there came another roar like the protest of the chair springs under the heft of a body too heavy for them. Before the loblolly trunk cracked at the base and shattered the sunroof, showering him with glass, the last thing Bub saw was his father sitting absolutely still, cradling his grandmother in his lap with her body strangely twisted so that both adults' faces turned toward the car under the descending pine tree. Yet the two pairs of glassy eyes seemed not to see the child in danger at all, but only to look inward at their own horror of the future as it hurtled every second toward them.

Reunion

In half-darkness, trees breathe like sleeping animals.
A cloud of low wings skims the dim lakescape,

their fluttering obscuring sounds of oars
breaking still water and our aimless chat

about our recklessness in school: rolling
your father's ATV jumping low hills

behind your house; nights driving through our town,
a paper cup of Coke and Southern Comfort

between our legs, a .45 stashed
in the glove box; driving blind down dirt roads.

And one time on a yellow, hot August noon
you lifted up a piece of scrap sheet metal

from tall late-summer grass to find beneath
a copperhead reared back to strike. You dropped

the metal, sprang a wild jumping dance
a good ten feet backwards, laughed. How are we

alive? And how are we still here, with twenty years
and more behind us, met again to sit

on this flat rock by this small lake,
almost like we were shipwrecked here,

almost like we were the survivors.

Decoration Day

We slice thick circles of bologna, lay
them on white bread beside the tilting grave
stones, to picnic with the dead. Beyond the fence
a mountain dams back open field where steers
drink muddy pond. We've come to pin down wreaths
of paper flowers, brought our old toothbrushes
to scrub the grooves that spell our lost ones' names.

This holiday was started for the rebel dead,
but now we come to clean the graves of all
our folk. In cemeteries through these hills
the Weed Eaters are whipping at pale stones
to clear the dandelion, henbit, poke
and years. There's not enough remembering
still.
           Now my 7-year-old daughter climbs
the low and lonely tree grown here and sits
against the light in thin top branches so
that when she calls I have to reach into
the sun to lift her down. I show her where
her people's graves lean each way out in line.
She tries to read the names. I try to teach
her. Family women stoop and touch the stones
with cleaning cloths, as gentle as the first
women some long millennia ago
to stoop and touch the rangy dogs that slinked
beyond the circled huts. I think these are
the rituals we've always used to tame
a wild, panting animal like grief.

Neglect

An orange-brown halo on the slab outside
  beside the cooling unit's bulk, a soil–
    and blood-smudged ring of rust around the pair
of needle-nosed pliers with which I tried
  to fix a leaking air conditioning coil.
    I left the thing unfixed. It got too cool to care.

The pliers are now flecked with the same turn
  to orange that's drained the trees of their green oil;
    they're both alight to show the year's unblinking stare,
aflame to show us how all things will burn
        in air.

Passing

The row of trees that marked the old fence line
was there to give us shelter from the wind.
The knobby oak, rough cedar, and tall pine,
a row of trees to hold the old fence line.
But even oaks will peak and then decline.
We watch the passing of our elder kin,
the row of trees that marked the old fence line
not there to give us shelter from the wind.

LESLEY CLINTON

Fallen Feather Stars

Crinoid Specimen, Houston Museum of Natural Science Hall of Paleontology

Feather-fanned, gossip-lipped, Mesozoic beauties
lean their heads whisper-close, crowding on some driftwood.
Land and mist bide their time, waiting for fresh life forms
to emerge from the sea, grow some legs, and wander,

but the wisps float on by, blithely filter feeding.
Heavenly looking things, they are quite at home here,
archetypal, blossoming in this warm beginning.
Slender-stemmed, giddy clique, they let currents tend them.

Were they to reach old age, palmy days would dwindle.
There'd be loss and decline but, too, metanoia.
Stars like these—brief and bright—never lose the shimmer
that eternity leaves on them when they're newly fashioned.

In short time, the branch grows waterlogged and sinks down,
leaving sun-clouded heights for anoxic, murky
depths. The stars fall to stone, ageless through the eons
till they're found fossilized, ancient in their newness.

Grief's Handiwork: An Allegory

After the illness struck,
those who lived near enough
gathered to bury the child.

The church doors sighed open;
the neighbors slipped
into the marbled blue night,

all but one, who stayed kneeling
till dawn, then appeared with the sun
at the young couple's home to assist

with the cooking and tending.
While they dined in silence
she piled plates and scrubbed pots

and mended socks. And she stayed on
through the patient adobe decades,
while the sun paled her blankets

and yarn hunched in baskets. A letter
with greening ink lay unread,
smooth in a mute box she kept

at her bedside. Now sun pries
at recesses. Doors shift. Light seeps in.
The lone guest, no longer guest,

works in the bleary light, threading
her faded strands into the form
of a midnight sunrise.

CHRISTIAN ANTON GERARD

Didn't Call for Rain

Folks here want to argue God cause folks don't know
what to say when there's nothing to be said; like how
we're standing around and it's raining, then raining hard,
then doing what might not fit rain's definition and it ain't

hail, but something all-together without words
and someone says how hard the rain is or stands there
saying it's raining like his brain don't know words except
it's and raining. Then someone says how nice it is to feel

something other than heat, how hot it was an hour ago.
Someone says the plants sure need it. Grass too. You hit
the streets, boys say all them worms come up from death
so the bass will bite, and your old man's friends will

head to Harry's for lunch tomorrow trying to say awe,
but it'll just be damn that was a storm last night.

Steady, I'm What They Call Expressive

It ain't that my hands are too heavy or full of blood
healing into new skin to lift past my waist
when we walk the tracks, it's that even talking
with my hands means our pinkies can't tie up

like the candy canes that calm me when I'm a rag-top
dropped, Wolfman Jack's trap flapping, nothing
but corn field after soy field and more stars than wild
in our hearts Friday night run out Route 30 past the strip.

My hands by my pockets is me trying not to talk
when there's nothing to say. Damn. I wish I could be
the errands need running, floors need cleaning. Hands
for driving. Counters need wiping. Hands to mouth. Hell,

I'll be whatever begs your hands without begging, being
needy. I know I got hands don't deserve your holding.

BRYAN HURT

Brain in a Jar

I'VE NEVER KNOWN NONA when she wasn't dying. Her cancer was like whack-a-moles; every time they got it, there it was popping up somewhere else. It was in her blood, her skin, her liver. "At least," she says, "it's not in my head. Brain cancer." She screws up her eyes and sticks out her tongue like a zombie. "BRAINS." She tells me her goal is to live until science figures out brains-in-jars technology. Then, at least, she'll be hermetically safe. "But with whom will I share an office?" I ask in the office that Nona and I have shared for the past six months. When they hired me here they told me that I'd get my own office, that the shared office was only temporary, but now I get the sense that it's my only office, and that my bosses are just waiting for Nona to die. Our desks meet in the middle of the room, which is white and windowless. All day, every day, we sit staring at our monitors. Staring at our monitors and also staring at each other, face-to-face. "You'll share it with the jar," she says. Her brown eyes and her brain floating in a tank. She says that it will be just like it is now but better. "Better," she says, "because no flesh bodies. Flesh bodies," she says. "Yuck." She says this and shivers because I know she's thinking about her cancer, the fucker of her body. Betrayer of her flesh. She turns the little plant that she keeps on her desk. The plant is a gift from her sister, designed to thrive in windowless offices, but to me it looks sick and yellow, always almost dying in the artificial light. Flesh bodies aren't all bad, though I don't say this to Nona. Instead I open an email and pretend to read while I think about Nona's flesh. Besides the rashes, the bruises, the skin that's sometimes yellow like an unripe grape, there's a lot to like about it. I like the brightly colored wraps she wears around her head after chemo. I like her swift, strong fingers. Her perfect posture at the computer. Her broad jaw and slim shoulders. I'd be lying if I didn't say I wasn't grateful that the cancer hasn't taken Nona's tits. Which is not to say that I have a crush on Nona. At least I don't think I do. To be honest, I'm not always good at knowing what I think. Like sometimes in a meeting when someone asks for my opinion, I'll open my laptop, click on a spreadsheet, and say, "hmm," like I'm having a thought and am looking for the words to express it. Most of the time people mistake this for a real idea. They call me the office intellectual and say that I'm deep. But in truth I'm the one who needs a brain in a jar. Some kind of hard and permanent shell to keep all of me together. It's like I walk around all day with a gusher on the top of my head. Nona sneezes. I look up from my spreadsheet and see that Nona's bleeding. A bright red line falls down her face. "Nona," I say and scramble for our Kleenex. But she knows too and is leaving. I sit there holding a tissue for a pair of legs and skirt that swishes out the door. Nona doesn't know it but some of us in the office have been making bets about her death. Alan across the hall says that she's got two more months to live. Meg the secretary gives her a year. Whenever we talk about it at the bar across the street after work, Jason, the office asshole, just says "tick, tick, tick." Everyone wants to know what I think, but when they ask me I just lift the beer up to my lips and feel the cool, hard glass in my fingers. The wet condensation, the reassuring heft. I know one day I'm going to come into my office and Nona won't be there. She'll leave and won't come back. I'll put away my lunch, close the door, and sit across from her empty desk. Maybe I'll go to the fountain and get some water for her plant. Maybe I'll turn it so it can get some light. Maybe I'll open Nona's filing cabinet and take her brain out of the drawer, all chrome and glass and pink muscle floating in clear suspension. I'll put her brain on my desk and tell her all the things I was scared to tell her. The things I've always been too scared to tell anyone else. "God, I've missed you," I'll say. "How was your weekend? My apartment was so empty. I finally killed my last plant." I'll ask her to tell me about dying. I was always so scared of her dying. I'm so scared of dying alone. I'll ask her to tell me what it was like. "Why didn't anyone tell us?" I'll ask. "Why didn't anyone tell us how hard it is to be alone?" Because at the end of the day that's all everyone is. Brains in jars floating though the liquid of our own existence. The best we can do is bump up against someone else's tempered dome. "I love you," I'll say for once in my life to someone. "I love you. I love you. I was just always too scared." I'll whisper these words into her insula, hoping that something penetrates the glass. I'll keep saying it until Jason knocks on my door and tells me it's time to leave the office. And then I'll go across the street and drink another beer.

MELISSA M. FRYE

Revelation in White Rock National Forest

Beads of light drip
through the canopy of leaves
and dapple the ground
like miniature spotlights
illuminating the path
to a lookout
where the full moon
shimmers on the tree-tops
sprawled below.
Here in the mountain air,
standing at the top of a cliff,
the night breeze cools my skin.
I am liberated.
Self-doubt crashes away.
I'm no longer peculiar,
no longer an outcast,
but rather a creation of God,
like the forest that surrounds me.

TIMOTHY KLEISER

Sowing Season

A farmer's come at autumn's ripened hour,
with goldenrod and aster still in bloom,
to amble under azure skies and shower
her furrowed field with garlic clove perfume.
To feed long love, to taste the summer birth
of Chesnok Reds and Susan Delafields,
she's come through years of quiet care and yields
again her silken secrets to the earth.

She's come alone, and yet she's not alone—
for there, within that hawthorn's mottled spray,
a spider weaves her silken sac, unknown
and unadored by every egg she'll lay
before she turns to die. For even she,
like some arachnid Archimedes, knows
her place upon the earth, then gladly goes
to sleep to dream of silk geometry.

Backyard Theology

These early springtime days—

when water maples cease
their silent vigil, shed
their sackcloth, and commence
in leafy decadence
to dance, as David did,
before the God of peace.

When humble worker bees
refrain from rationing
their precious honey stock
and leave their hive to gawk
at how harsh snows could bring
them flowers such as these.

When warbler scouts forget
their fear of falcon wings
and resurrect their nests
while summoning their best
vibrato just to sing,
"already, but not yet."

When she, my flesh and blood,
while climbing toward the sun,
is spooked by some bird's caw
and proves Sir Newton's law,
then I, a sinner, run
to kiss away the mud.

—I know that God is love.

Burying a Racehorse

Beyond the vacant hoof-hewn trails, across
the fields, upon the hillside stretching like
a wave above a sea of aftergrass,
their shovels pierce and pitch the stony earth.

With steady, practiced strokes, they toil to pull
away the pennyroyal quilts, to rouse
the crumbling limestone from its crider bed,
and make a paddock-grave upon this spot.

There won't be talk of fire—no matter what
it costs in strain and sweat, no matter how
the bigger farms may treat their dead. No flame
should taste what's owed to earth—and so they dig.

The horses here are born to strike the ground
forevermore. So now this soil will be her
saddle, these ancient stones her shoes, to race
In pennyroyal silks of purple-green.

GEFFREY DAVIS

Arkansas Aubade

—after "Untitled (Throwblankets)," by Pete Driessen

One grief, all morning—: it finally matters where
in the body we choose to hang
        our turn: too high & no emotional

legacy longer than loss throws down
against the laden light. It takes risk
        & a bloodier precision to ring the next psalm

from the other side of our survival:—
another venous truth torqued
        from the crimson length of memory.

Pleasures of Place

You are this kind of wonder in the dark, Dear Boy:
I have spent the evening on our porch, smoking
in quiet complaint, comparing old pleasures of places
I have lived—how we leave behind something vital,
and know the fact once we catch its absence
broadcasted by new towns.

                              Inland Oregon made me
miss the shoreline—the salty endlessness
of the rocks barnacled along Commencement Bay.
Then I despised the low rise of the Allegheny Ridge,
which was another way of remembering the West,
of registering my loss of Mt. Hood, and Mt. Rainier
before that—their constant loom no longer
fixing me from the horizon.

                              And tonight it's the thinness
of these Arkansas fireflies, learning me just how flooded with light
our Pennsylvania yard became.

                              As if on cue, you come
bombing out the backdoor, two flashlights in hand, and run
deep into the August dark, where you invent a dazzling
dance that frames your body in this turning I can't describe.
From beyond an Ozark oak, I know you—:
the erasure of my face lit brilliant by the country
of your presence.

GEFFREY DAVIS

It is no small thing to discover fresh words for old wounds.*

M EMORY, faith, form, safety, silence, truth . . . the things I
have tried to ransom for a love story that might out sing
the fears and facts otherwise threatening those I hold dear. This
poem stumbles narratively and lyrically toward some chance to
give one of my most troubled family faces a new name. It is no
small thing to discover fresh words for old wounds. In doing so,
we invite alternate, healthy ways of understanding our survival; in
doing so, we intercede for the impossible connections in which we
desire and deserve to be alive.

* * *

This is also the oldest piece in my first collection (a book that takes
its name from this poem), the one that just won't seem to leave me
alone. In fact, the poem has been reincarnated across my entire
writing life. Each time I discover a version I think will let me move
on, I turn around and recognize its troubled voice asking me again
to rethink how I've got it all wrong, how writing it down (and all

---

* This essay was originally published in *Poetry Northwest* (March 2018) with
the title poem of Geffrey Davis's first collection, *Revising the Storm* (2014). The
author has graciously allowed us to reprint the essay here, and we encourage you
to read the poem as well.

its previous iterations) was never going to satisfy or realize—what? I'm failing sometimes to even know what it is that I'm praying for.

* * *

When I ignite what I believe to be this poem's fuse, the imaginative momentum flounders at take off—no boom. Honestly, I think that's why the current version is in sections, why it keeps doubling back for a new way to move toward something resembling light. And suddenly, I hope this poem's failure to launch also says something about its integrity, though I can't be sure. Lately, in my own reading, I've been less interested in a poem's *positive* integrity—how it can confirm or prove what it has come to tell us. Instead, I find myself utterly demolished (in the best way) by a poem that strains into its *negative* integrity—how it hates but must finally admit the limits or uncertainty of everything it has come to tell us—no matter how deeply or dearly we pray for the next beat or note that might further unlock the human condition. When we experience that kind of poem, one where failure is in the marrow of the voice, we learn to rest inside the alert of failure, to ponder not against but according to the sighs of the ineffable.

* * *

[If you're reading this, I'm trying my best to love you.]

* * *

I've lucked into many wonderful poetry mentors. Failure guides, if you will. One such figure is the poet Todd Davis. Before I even began publishing, he was the first to explicitly invite me to tune out the broader noise of public reception. He suggested instead that one should attend more to the local, body-to-body impact of putting poems into the world, to watch how our everyday communities react with our poems in their mouths. And that's the breakdown I find myself flailing inside of the most these days, especially as I'm putting my second collection to bed (a book that, in many ways, picks up where the first one stumbled off). In the end, I wrote and rewrote "Revising the Storm" to diminish the space and silence growing between loved ones and me—and it didn't work, not like I've been begging it to. For all the ways in which poetry has been responsible for the best survival(s) of my life, I can't help but fixate on those loves that I haven't yet figured out how to (mis)understand. And maybe that's just a differently necessary relationship to failure, one I'm only beginning to learn about. But in the meantime, they're still slipping away, their presences thinning, their lovely voices making it less clearly to my ever-more-distant ears.

* * *

[If you're reading this, I'm trying my best to be here.]

* * *

. . . *breath, body, belonging, rest*: I have come so far on the back of poetry. I have so much work left within this life not yet saved.

three divine faces, in the style of emily.

I.

no emerald can outshine the duck
nor ruby the winecup's curl.
Nature humbles every gem
but you, my Love, are her pearl.

II.

spring will come to texas when
soil blackens, a moonless hour—
then Nature dips Her slender pen
and scrawls Her cursive wildflowers.

III.

there's a rainbow you cannot view,
i hid it in a clouded sky—
i hope one day that gray will part
so you see it before i die.

cauldron.

grandmother cast iron is the best
everyone knows that but i don't have any
hers rusted in one of the hurricanes
i can't remember which one,

i lost track of my storms.

       so

i make do with a new pan i try my best
even though the grip is love unsmoothed
and it gets too hot too fast
and it refuses to hold seasoning
and it snaps at raw meat and holds
for
         dear life.

maybe after eighteen years of
my rainbowed fingers my tallowed palms
maybe one
            night

the wet will take
settle into the metal
weed any lingering rust flowers
leaving only violet black.

can't say i blame the iron, though—
can't say that i do.

i know what it is to want something
so badly
that you're willing to
burn.

GLORIA WILLIAMS TRAN

Clapboard House

Fleeing the crowds and clamor of L.A.,
we escaped to the Central Valley,
rented a white clapboard farmhouse
fifteen miles from town.
An idyllic setting, we said,
beside a pasture with two horses,
cows in the field out front,
and a creek behind us with wild fig trees.

Tim got a job at the junkyard
down the road, dismantling autos
while dodging black widows
that lodged in the rusting bodies of cars.
I stayed home and played housewife
and mother to his ten-year-old girl
who rode the school bus every day
to a hamlet peopled, we later
learned, by druggies.

Our city cat, scared of cows, stayed indoors,
so we got a litter to combat rats in the barn.
On good days I walked across the pastures
to follow the creek bed, then back along
a country road, hoping to spy someone
to pass a word or two. I took up crafts,
decorating cut-up toilet paper tubes,
a magazine's idea for Christmas napkin rings.

A year of that life was enough.
Shedding our back-to-the-land dreams,
our second-hand furniture, and my mother's teacups,
we drove away from the yellowed summer fields
in two '57 Chevies with our cat and daughter,
midway across the continent to land
in a small Southern town called Paris,
lush with verdant lawns and pink mimosa blooms,
to live again in a white clapboard house.

Autumn Duo

Tall slender stalks of okra
sway in the autumn breeze.
Dead fronds fallen away,
only a few skinny leaves remain.

Creamy blossoms with magenta hearts
fold and curl inward forming
ribbed pods of sticky white seeds,
gathered for my supper.

Like the okra stalks I pick,
I stand slightly bent with age,
slicing each pod from its stem,
hoping for yet another harvest.

JIM BEAUGEZ

The Dog Hunter

E DWARD NODDED AWAKE when the tires crunched on gravel and the truck eased to a stop. Pops grabbed the perforated yellow cards with their names and address scribbled over the lines and dropped them in the box at the check-in post. Then he spun the truck back onto the river road with one palm rotating the wheel and kept to the center, dodging holes and the washboard runoff ruts along the edges.

Pops turned onto a nameless slag-and-clay road, then another, and followed it around a bend. A few dozen yards ahead, the headlights caught the back end of a tailgate at the turnoff. He tapped the brakes, but then continued up the road and stopped at the beat-up Silverado parked in the weeds. Inside the bed, a pair of mangled cages sat obscured in shadows.

"Dammit."

"You wanna try another place?" Edward asked, blinking slowly and rubbing his forehead.

"Nah. This is the one." Pops threw the transmission into reverse and goosed the accelerator, looking over his shoulder all the way, then backed into the clearing and shut off the truck. He grabbed his travel mug out of the cup holder. "There's one path in from here, but it splits off to trails ever' now and again. We're headin' toward a food plot in the back. Don't want anyone huntin' on top of us."

Pops was meticulous in his planning and not easily deterred. He had mapped this spot weeks ago in anticipation of a quick Thanksgiving morning hunt while Edward was on fall break. In deer season his kitchen table became a war room of relief maps, holes worn into the folds from years of use. Piles of camouflage clothing to anticipate every conceivable combination of terrain, temperature, and precipitation. Boxes of expended brass casings in the corner of the room.

Edward reached into his shirt pocket and pulled out half of a peanut butter and grape jelly sandwich, unwrapped it, and set it on the dash. Pops handed him the thermos and smirked in the dark cab as his son's hands struggled to get enough grip to torque the worn cap.

After a few adjustments, the pressure hissed and the seal broke.

"'Bout time." Pops smiled a short grin out the corner of his mouth, eyes fixed toward the night.

Edward poured a cup and chewed his sandwich slowly as he sat half awake. He still felt weak from the nap he'd taken on the drive. With the dash lights off, his eyes adjusted as the night began its slow fade into dawn. He could just make out the top of the tree line above hulking shapes that would soften into patches of kudzu by first light. If he concentrated on one spot, it would appear to grow before his eyes like a Rorschach blob. He had no faith in the dark.

In the slow spaces between thoughts, Edward sipped the coffee Pops had prepared earlier in the morning. It was a process with him. First he prepped the thermos with boiling water while the coffee percolated. Then he added some milk, some sweetener, to the coffee. Back to near boiling in the microwave, finally into the thermos.

"Good coffee," Edward said. "I guess it should be, as long as it takes you to make it." Three o'clock in the morning was too early for him, but everything with Pops started with an early rise, it seemed. Although lately Pops didn't have to set an alarm. Getting older did that, he'd told him.

"Here. Put these in your pockets."

He took the warming packets from Pops and set them on his lap. It wasn't especially cold when they'd left town, but down in the bayou the air always felt chillier.

Edward couldn't see the first light peeking over the horizon for the cover of the swamp, but he looked at his watch and knew it was coming. Pops turned off the dome light and opened the door slowly, dulling the squeak and skronk of the hinges. He reached behind the seat and slid his rifle out of its case. Edward followed, the familiar smell of 3-in-One Oil hitting him as he loaded .30-06 shells into the magazine of the gun Pops had brought for him to use.

"Here." Edward handed him a two-way radio. "Just like I showed you. Keep the volume low. It's set to channel 5." Pops finally had a cell phone, but he hardly kept it on and never texted. Wouldn't matter down here anyway, Edward figured. Some places in the lowlands were still remote enough that nothing could find them. Pops clipped the radio to his pullover and shouldered his rifle like a soldier heading into the bush.

"Alright, let's ease off."

The dark earth bore their footfalls along the old logging road. Edward could just make out his father's lumbering outline in front of him, as though an apparition morphing in a heavy fog, until it grew more definite in the purplish early dawn. They slowed now, stalking the inside of curves with patience and intent, watching for antlers or flashes of white, any muted change in the pattern of the woods.

Pops usually preferred the hills upriver, where he could follow the ridgelines into sloughs and find game trails along the natural funnels. Down here, just off the path, stilled waters crept onto land when the tide entered the swamp. The water's edge waited like a trap, blurring any separation between the solid and the infinite. Persistent winter rains and summer hurricanes left their marks on the trunks of cypress and live oaks where the water table rose and then receded. With the flatness and low cover of yaupons, Edward thought, a logging road will do just fine.

"That's a good spot there," Pops whispered, stopping to point out a slight rise along the path just beyond the next curve. They hugged the inside edge on their approach with knees bent and heads lowered. Then, satisfied there was nothing around the corner, they stood upright and kept walking.

"Now, I don't know we'll see anything." Pops paused and looked up and down the road. "But this spot, you can see 'em from a couple different ways. As good as any place in here."

Pops turned toward the landscape ahead in the early light. Just beyond them, mounds of disheveled dirt and leaves pocked the path before it meandered around another corner. "And if you see a hog, plug it. No limit on those bastards."

Edward leaned the rifle against the embankment and worked to unclip a folding seat from his belt loop.

"I'm gonna keep walking a-ways," Pops said, tapping the two-way with his forefinger. "Catch ya on the radio." Then he set off.

Edward turned and climbed the sandy mound as his father receded in the graying morning light, gliding through the dead grass, avoiding the crunch and snap of fallen leaves and twigs littering the ground. Now alone, he wedged his seat between two white oaks for cover. Then he sat and waited. In the idle silence, he imagined a thorny eighteen-inch rack emerging from the yaupons broadside. The deer turned, squaring to him like the outline on the targets he used. The perfect shot.

Deer rarely grew that big down here along the coast. He'd put down any good-sized doe or legal buck that wandered his way. He gazed forward and thought about the first deer he'd killed, a little button buck, a single shot from that .30-06 dead center. He had meant to shoot the legal deer but lost him as the two danced around a doe. The one that peeked from behind a pine tree looked straight at him. That should've been Edward's clue. He steadied the crosshairs but never heard the rifle fire or felt the recoil. The deer sprinted forty yards before collapsing in spasms.

Pops made the first incision once they'd hung the buck head-down from a rope they had hoisted over the first heavy branch. The oak limb sagged under the weight, so Edward had to untie the rope, stretch it tighter and then tie it to a pine sapling ten yards away. The deer's skin and hide peeled reflexively from the cut. Pops began to slash with precision along the left flank, pulling away from the carcass with his left hand while working the blade with his right. Edward held the animal in place and studied his father's technique.

"Your turn," Pops said, passing the knife to his son. The hide hung from one side, bunching at the neck. A small pool of blood had collected on the ground where it dripped from the muzzle.

Edward held the knife in his grip, shuffling his stance and repositioning for the awkward job. The deer twisted and bumped him as he figured out the rhythm of this animal that had been alive only moments before, until he'd caught him in his scope. He didn't know how to feel about it, so he focused on finishing the job in silence.

The slender blade nicked at the hide as he pulled, and it began to drop in sheets once he fell into a groove. All the skin and connective tissue layered in concert yielded easily to him now. He worked along the abdomen, slicing and peeling, following the course of the sinew around the shoulder and down the spine. Finally, the hide hung like a hood over the buck's head, leaving the carcass exposed, deep red meat under the sheen of silver skin.

Pops took the knife and traced the outline of the lower abdominal cavity, careful not to puncture the membranous sac holding its intestines. Then he separated them and pulled out the sac, dropping it onto the pile of unusable flesh. Noxious steam rose from the carcass and the entrails, and they were thankful it would cool quickly in the cold morning air.

* * *

Edward's thoughts were broken by distant barking—staccato bursts of primal fury piercing the solitude of the morning. Assholes, he thought, as he tried to gauge direction and distance. It was difficult to tell in the dense swampland. They seemed to be getting closer, and he knew they would be there soon.

He grabbed his radio and felt for the knobby red button.

"You hear that? Bastards think they own this place." Then he waited.

"Yeah." Pops's voice came through softer than he expected, a determined whisper, after a moment of dead air.

"Where are they?"

"Not too far from me. Maybe three hundred yards east, past the trees on the other side of the food plot."

"What do you want to do?"

"Wait."

But Edward already feared how this would go. He felt it in his stomach, suddenly hollow and sour. The dogs would push closer, possessed by the scent of fear in the woods. It wouldn't be long until the locals showed up with buckshot. The anger and fear and anticipation gnawed at him. He was sure the dogs were closer now, as his eyes scanned from one curve to the other on the logging road before him. He wiped his palms on his pants and swallowed hard.

Pops broke the silence. "They're pullin' in. Ain't seen what they're chasin' yet. No hunters either. You see anyone walkin' the road?"

Edward surveyed the roadbed again. Winter-yellowed grasses covered the old tire ruts, just slight depressions now in the ground. He gripped the rifle on his lap as he held guard.

"Nobody yet."

Edward sat still, upright and alert, for what seemed an interminable wait while the dogs closed the distance toward Pops. The yelps grew sharper in pitch and shorter in length, the cacophony pausing and changing direction as they lost and found game trails across cypress sloughs, marching again through muted undergrowth along rises lifting out of the water's reach.

Edward steeled himself for a fight. This land may have belonged to your granddaddy, he imagined himself saying, but it's not yours. Everyone with a license has a right to hunt here. He could see that son of a bitch now. The kind he might find on a Friday night at any crossroads tavern up here. The one over by the paper mill, or the creosote plant upriver.

"I see 'em now." Edward could hear them under his father's voice. "Four. No, five. Shit, the big one made me."

The radio went silent again but the ravenous barking in the distance grew louder.

"They're all on me." Pop's voice was more urgent now, but still in control. "I got nowhere to go. Gonna hafta shoot to get outta here."

"No!" Edward blurted, fumbling with the radio. Killing a dog would only escalate the situation. "See who shows up to call them off."

CRACK went the first shot. Then a pause. And then came the CRACK again. He felt vertigo from his intentions leaving his body and the involuntary jittering of his muscles, the terror of confrontation. He couldn't sit any longer. He rose in slow motion and his legs moved like hunks of timber. His arms no longer did what he wanted them to do and his rifle slipped from his grip.

CRACK! This time deafening and immediate and blinding.

Edward toppled over his seat and lunged forward through the low scrub, shoved as if by an unseen hand into the damp earth at the bottom of the rise. He searched frantically for the source of the sound that had stopped the world and brought it rushing back to him ten times louder and faster. Scrambling to his knees amid the chaos in his head, Edward pushed down with his left hand and felt his strength yield, the surprise and pain coursing through his body and out his mouth. His eyes followed the pain to his shoulder, where deep red blood had soaked through his layers. He rolled to his right side and propped himself up. Then he ripped off his blaze orange vest and wrapped it around his left shoulder, tying the thin fabric down tight with one hand and his teeth. He shuddered again when the pressure hit the bullet wound and the world began to tilt. Staggering upright, finding his feet as if for the first time, Edward grabbed his rifle and set out in the direction he'd last seen his father, where the gunshots had blasted and now he heard nothing.

Bright sunlight from a cloudless sky cast daytime shadows from narrow trees across the path. Edward wandered through them: light to dark, light to dark. He crossed the roadbed instinctively as it twisted, never quite feeling his footfalls or knowing reality from dream, except for the searing pain that shot through his body with each movement. His legs jerked in an awkward gait toward what he didn't know but feared more than his own condition, so that he was compelled against his own preservation.

Edward stared hard forward as he pushed himself down the trail, as ready as he could be to meet the dogs or his father or someone coming toward him. The woods lay still around him, but his mind flitted through distracting thoughts of a life that was becoming more distant as the blood soaked his jacket. He had walked nearly a quarter mile when the trail got messy. He slopped through an intersection of hoof marks moving in all directions, the soupy gray mud sucking at his boots, pulling him down, when a flash of color caught his eye through the trees. Edward reached for a low branch and used it to pull himself upright and then craned his neck, peering under the canopy until he caught the orange fabric again and made a path toward it.

"Pops!" Edward reached for his father, who was bundled on the ground, face down, at the edge of the clearing. "Pops!" He made no movement of his own, so Edward rolled him over and a panicked wail escaped from his throat when he saw the exit wound on his forehead.

Life and death and grief and fear hit Edward at once as he clutched his father by the coat, eyes locked in terror. There was no yesterday or tomorrow, no swapping stories back at the truck of the doe he couldn't manage to shoot, no ride back to town knowing the comfort and warmth that waited to greet them. No beer and a lounger and meat on the grill. No fireflies or football. No confiding and no confidence at all and no future except this one. Panic gripped him in the silent morning. Edward searched for Pops's keys but they were gone, as were his radio and his gun. His throbbing shoulder pain resurfaced as he stared into the face of his father, an expression frozen in one moment of horror, and began moving away. Away from it all.

Edward spun around and took off in a sprint, then hesitated and changed direction, hesitated again and looked back to his father, now fifty yards through the trees, motionless. The fear and adrenaline and blood loss made his body an agitated, nervous mess and he overflowed with all the anger and fear and hurt surging through his body. He had to find a way out, to get back on high ground and get his father out of the swamp. He had to get out before they found him, but the thoughts that had come ten at a time now felt distant, as if filtered through the old tube television set his father never gave up. He stumbled off, directionless into trees that all looked the same, weaving through them in fits, his legs finally wrapping under his body and dragging him down next to the slough where the mirrored water stole onto land.

* * *

The afternoon sunlight glinted through the opening in the canopy and pierced Edward's right eye as he buried his left in the coarse weave of his twill camouflage jacket. He squinted and sighed, the puff of vapor spreading a pocket of warmth across his face in the cold air.

He lay on his side, keeping pressure on his shoulder. The sunlight warmed him in the places where it hit him. The warmth and the nausea: they reminded him of the first sensation of bleeding, the moment following the moment he had felt the slug's impact. He curled his knees to his chest and shivered. In that quiet, so vacuous he thought he could hear the presence and density of the air around him, his radio crackled to life, pushing his stomach into his throat. Blood coursed through him like a caged animal and adrenaline filled his veins. Finally, a voice.

"Hellllll-o? What we got here?" The dry, raspy rattle paused. Edward's pulse quickened. "Anybody home?"

Edward fumbled the radio. As he tried to stabilize it, he inadvertently triggered the talk button, flashing a momentary signal of static over the airwaves. Edward wished like hell he could have that moment back.

"Well, now." The voice was weathered, but matter-of-fact and sober. "Now listen, I wanna talk to you. Seems we got a little business to settle."

Edward lay still in the pocket of underbrush where he landed, how long ago he couldn't say.

"You gonna man up and talk?"

Edward cursed himself.

"All right then. I guess you know you trespassin'. Goddamn poachers. Oughta string you up like we used to do—"

"The fuck's the matter with you?" Edward shouted into the radio. "This ain't your land!"

"You done screwed up. Your daddy, he ain't gettin' up. He ain't goin' nowhere. And once them hogs catch a whiff . . . hell, maybe a gator. Or even some dogs. Right, boys? Y'all gonna eat good today." The chorus of sharp, cackling barks swallowed the man's voice.

"We eat what we kill. Whatcha know 'bout that?" His hacking laughter hung in the air after the radio went silent.

Edward writhed inside his muddy camouflage. The dampness reached into his bones, and when the wind blew it chilled through his wound straight to his core. He popped the snap on a black leather sheath and drew his knife, examined the blade, and tried to imagine himself digging out the .30-06 slug to build up the nerve to do it. Not yet, he thought as bile jumped into his throat. He slid it along his calloused fingertips, the black halos of mud outlining his fingernails, and began to dig at them methodically, his mind hovering somewhere overhead like a blanket of fog that hung heavy over the swamp, here but not, dreamlike and dazed. A deep red speck on his index finger grew into a bulb and dripped onto the ground.

Thoughts rolled around Edward's mind, so real he could see them play out in front of him. If he waited where he was, eventually the dogs would track him here. He could try for solid ground and wade through the sloughs to diffuse his scent as he moved toward what he thought was the highway. Not a whole lot else seemed reasonable. But he didn't want to run. He knew no matter what he did, only one of them was going to leave this swamp.

His heartbeat pulsed in his ears, swallowing all other sound as his shoulder throbbed in rhythm with the blood coursing through him. He grabbed a tree limb with his good arm, then pulled himself up and began picking his way around cypress knees. He found a narrow rise and dragged along a game trail through young white oaks. Water-logged acorns popped under his boots and wispy bare limbs swatted him along the way. His eyes swept from one side to another, scanning for patches of upturned earth on the slopes to his left and right. Where the trail leveled back down to the lowland, he stumbled into a hog rut as wide as a two-lane highway.

Stinking mounds of upturned mud had been rooted up from the swamp, with leaves and grass crisscrossing the bottom where the trail widened. A line of pines along the edge bore the scars of repeated rubbing, most of them worn past the bark and now stained the color of ash. He eased through the slop and slumped under a live oak whose low branches reached onto the path. The understory here, bare except for the carpet of old leaves, gave him a place to rest.

Edward propped his rifle against the trunk and eased himself down between two root ridges. He leaned his head back against the tree. In the canopy above him, a dense network of finger-like leaves and spindly Spanish moss reached down toward him on the ground. As he worked to slow his breathing, he eyed his surroundings. On the opposite side of the trail, the understory thickened about forty yards into the hardwoods, up a slope toward higher ground.

Then movement caught his eye. In the clearing, a tan-white tuft the color of the dead winter grass bobbed. As it drew closer, Edward thought it was a yearling and raised his scope to get a better look, pressing the rifle stock against his right shoulder. Opportunity waits for no man, his father had often said. This was his.

Edward focused the crosshairs just behind the young deer's left shoulder and squeezed the trigger. The gun jumped with recoil, sending an agonizing tremor through his torso. The deer dropped and kicked wildly, pushing itself across the blanket of leaves. Edward ambled to his feet, steadied his aim and fired one more round, this time puncturing the jugular and a mass of arteries in the deer's neck and sending spurts of blood to soak the ground.

He waited for the twitching to stop. Then he crept out from under the edge of the leaf cover and walked to the deer, nudging it with his boot. He kicked it over and examined the red, matted hair in the middle of its abdomen. A pungent smell wafted up and seared his nostrils. Gut shot. He took a hind leg in his right hand and struggled to pull the undersized deer into the ruts, stopping mid-stride to catch his breath. Then he threaded his knife from the animal's neck through its abdomen and spilled the mess on the ground.

Edward wiped his knife on his pants and slid back underneath the branches, settling himself into his spot with his back against the trunk. He drew up his right knee, laid the forestock of his rifle over it, and trained his scope on the yearling. A light north wind wicked at his cheeks and he shook off waves of discomfort left by his cooling sweat. He exhaled a long breath like he would if he were pulling the trigger and felt what remained of his emotions vaporize.

Reaching into the folds of his jacket, he pulled out a grunt call, drew it to his cracked lips, and blew. With his eyes looking downwind toward the undergrowth deep inside the tree cover, he hit the call again, waited a minute, and blew once more.

Without uttering a sound, a large sow broke through the tangled growth and charged into the clearing, headed straight for Edward's tree. As he had hoped, the smell diverted her attention and she grunted and whined as she tore into the deer. A succession of smaller pigs followed in a line and all but disappeared behind the animal's abdomen, where they ripped smaller pieces of flesh.

The din of the hogs nearly covered the sound of the approaching pack. As they came into Edward's view, the alpha muscled ahead, his jowls peeled back behind ivory incisors like a deranged smile, eyes wild in pursuit. The blitzkrieg broke formation to surround the pigs, gnashing and barking, challenging the feral hogs. The sow bolted at the alpha, goring his neck and gnawing as she drove him to the ground. With the mother occupied, the pack swarmed the smaller, defenseless hogs. The squealing and whining faded into whimpering as the dogs subdued them all.

The sow charged again, and the two danced around the bloody pile, sparring under the soft glow of dusk as the low winter sun eased behind the trees. The lesser dogs snapped for a mouthful of flesh, tearing into her tough skin but unable to get a firm grip. She continued driving the alpha backward through the mud with little concern for the pack tearing away at her legs and hind. Just as the dogs began to pull her down, Edward heard the familiar CRACK CRACK reverberate across the swamp, and the sow dropped.

He never heard him approach and had no idea how long he'd been watching the carnage. But now he saw the gangly man working along the tree line toward them, rifle slung low but ready to shoulder. Mismatched camouflage hung off his long limbs, a sunken face with stringy dark hair draped over a taut neck. His eyes were the most striking feature—two dark, intense orbs bulging from gaunt sockets that swept back and forth across the cold dead ground. He recognized the strap stretched across his chest, holding a second rifle across his back. It had belonged to Pops.

A warm sensation ran down the back of Edward's neck, and his stomach turned. Suddenly he felt exposed under his tree, but he couldn't risk moving. There was no way to do it without giving away his position. But when he looked back at the man, he was no longer standing there. In just a few moments, Edward had lost his target to the swamp, and his sure shot vanished. Fearing he'd surrendered the upper hand, his panic intensified and his grip grew sweaty. He put his right eye to the scope and tried to steady the barrel so he could get a better look. At what, he didn't know. He had no clue which direction the man had moved, or if he saw Edward and was setting up his own shot.

Edward pulled back the bolt on his rifle to make sure he had chambered a round, then eased off the safety and moved into a prone position on the ground, favoring his good side. He felt safer at ground level. Twenty yards away, the dogs smacked and snarled, bloodied muzzles rising and returning to their kill, over and over. Edward unsheathed his blade and set it on the ground next to him.

Before every move he made, deep within, he performed the mental calculus that weighed cause and effect, and risk and reward, until there was nothing left to resolve. When the man emerged from behind the trees across the path, Edward no longer had to think or feel. Sliding his finger inside the trigger guard, he exhaled and pulled.

The Moon Lives Here

When I was six, we moved from west Texas
to Oklahoma, and I was so excited to see the dirt.

I kept hearing, over and over, that it was red.
That it was clay. That it stained everything.
My mother seemed afraid of it,
but to me it sounded like magic.
In west Texas, the dirt was a pale gray dust,
and grew no trees.

I made my grandma tell me the names of Oklahoma trees
over the phone, because their names sounded like a magic spell:
Redbud, Blackjack, Cottonwood, Soapberry, Dogwood.
And I would repeat them back to myself falling asleep at night.

When we arrived, I left to find the magic earth.
It stained everything, as advertised.
When I asked why it was this color, my mom said,
"It has a lot of iron—the same thing that makes blood red."

In third grade, we learned about the Trail of Tears,
and I thought, "That's why the dirt is red in Oklahoma."
I was too young yet to have learned about atrocities committed
all over the world, but I would come in time to wonder about the color of the dirt
in Auschwitz and Nagasaki and Cambodia and Nigeria, too.

One night in the parking lot after church, just seven then,
I stood with the teenagers admiring the Harvest Moon,
rising strange and red into the night sky. One of the boys,
standing on someone's car hood, said, "There's blood on the moon tonight!"

But I knew. It wasn't blood. It was red dirt.
The moon rose up from Oklahoma.

Family Trees

Tom Waits said,
"My mother was a tree."

Yes. Bring a hammer and hook
and suspend from her a hammock.
Or with a spile and drill,
drain from her straight syrup.

My father was the laugh I caught
when I pierced myself. "I'm fine,"
I said, bleeding through my fingers,
licking iron, painting handprints
on doorways, cut from trees:

The Christ is coming,
have you heard?
If I am not a tree,
he might be me.

But if I leaf out in darkness—
if I bleed sweetness
like my mother—
            you hang him on me.

GERRY SLOAN

Searching for Muscadines

*"The smell and taste of things remain poised a long time, like souls, ready to
remind us, waiting and hoping for their moment, amid the ruins of all the rest."*
—*Marcel Proust,* Remembrance of Things Past

For the first time in years
my father appears to me in a dream
though I forget what he said or did.
But I remember the flavor
of wild grapes foraged
over sixty years ago
at the foot of Rich Mountain,
my redneck madeleine,
though clueless about Proust
at the time.
                    But the taste
of muscadines has stayed with me,
summoning another summer Sunday,
Dad's only day off, after his favorite
breakfast of bacon and eggs
fried over easy, a gargantuan leap
from French cookies dipped in tea
to dairy-fresh milk and biscuits
with a dollop of hillbilly jelly.

How many miles south of our house
on the outskirts of town, a house
long since torn down? And what
was that taste he conjured
from the tangle of vines
tucked under some shade,
plucked and placed on my tongue
as if by magic, even sweeter than
Grapette soda or Concord grapes?

It's a quest as much as a question now
as the seasons continue on their rounds.
If you should someday find me wandering
distractedly by a rural fence-row, please
think of this poem and know I haven't
entirely lost my mind, Dad still out there
somewhere, guiding me to the ripest ones.

JACK B. BEDELL

Tracks, Dugdemona River

Follow your dog along this soft bank
     long enough and you'll see

all manner of prints—
     water birds, whitetail deer,

otter. Most follow the same path
     you're on, headed downstream

in the shade. Some will still be
     fresh enough to draw

the dog's nose right into the mud;
     some will have been

pressed next to this river
     forever. It's best to let

the dog decide how long
     you linger at each mark.

Should it find any tracks
     facing toward or away

from the water, it'll most likely
     balk at their thick smell

and rush back to heel.
     Those deep prints

should always be left to themselves
     before they leave a mark on your day.

Swamp Thing Contemplates a Heel Turn

Just once, I'd love to look the other way when two hikers get stuck in the silt trying to cross the swamp on their way to self-enlightenment, to just stay in the shade when I hear a scream echo from across the bay. I mean, imagine how fantastic it would feel to be Ted DiBiase turning his back on Dick Murdoch, his mentor's hand groping toward the corner for a tag. Or Larry Zbyszko putting his boot right between Bruno Sammartino's shoulder blades when the champ spun around to wave to his adoring fans. It would be so sweet to belly laugh at that crowd and stretch a slow grin from underneath my diablo mask. And Parts Unknown. Man, what a cool, dry place to stay that would be.

Swamp Lessons

I. Whatever It Is,
It Already Knows You're Here

My uncle taught me
not to fear noises
in the swamp. Nothing
that wants your blood
will make a sound.

II. Never Want What's Left Behind

There are no good reasons
for a house to be abandoned
in the swamp. Let it sink
into the mud. Nothing
in its shadows is worth
the claws of memory.

III. These Woods Will Tell You
What You Need to Know

Listen to the knocks they make at night.
Notice the claw marks high up
on the trees surrounding camp,
prints along the river.
Keep to the clearing.
Trust your nose.

Swamp Thing Ruminates on a Line from Thomas Merton

Your life is shaped by the end you live for. You are made in the image of what you desire. The first time I heard this, I was holed up in the palmettos behind Our Lady of Blind River waiting for the sun to drop so I could move on. There was a woman inside the chapel chanting Merton, and it all seemed to square with the world to the left and right of me. Because I was sitting in the shade hungry, it sounded like standard nutritional advice, actually. Clean fuel in, clean energy out, you know. You are what you eat kind of stuff. I mean, the poule d'eau diving for fish in the water behind me tasted like fish, the choupique nosing silt tasted like mud, so it made sense then. Looking at my own reflection on the bayou now, though, I'm starting to realize Merton was herding us more toward the zen of desire with all that stuff. My whole grown life, I've been alone in a lab chasing God, trying to make something out of nothing like He did. I never wanted to BE God. That was never my goal. I wanted to be as God is to this world, a provider, someone who could turn stone into bread or desert into paradise so we could all share in it. And look at me now. There is nothing in this whole swamp more consubstantial than I am—all dirt and vine and anger and guilt. Infinitely so, in the image of my desire.

Sour Grapes

"The word of the Lord came to me: What do you mean by repeating this proverb concerning the land of Israel, 'The parents have eaten sour grapes, and the children's teeth are set on edge'? As I live, says the Lord God, this proverb shall no more be used by you in Israel."

—Ezekiel 18:2–3 (NRSV)

Edmund Ruffin—long stringy white hair, something out of a vainglorious middle-aged self-portrait, the man who fired the first shot of the Civil War—is dead. Dead by his own rifle. I don't much care if it was the same rifle he used at Fort Sumter.

Jubal Early is dead, fallen down a flight of stairs. It's one of those things that's not funny but it kind of is. That little general raided Maryland and gave them such a scare up in Washington. And there he lay at the bottom of a bunch of stairs, the man who brought destruction to Thaddeus Stevens's gates.

James Earl Ray is dead, dead as the booming-voiced King—the dreamer he slew—died pleading his innocence like most everybody else in prison. Strom Thurmond, the old Dixiecrat senator, is dead at one hundred years, his sins pardoned for reaching such a ripe old age.

And my great-grandfather is dead; his liver failed in 1924. He was a civil engineer. "I hope to be drunk by noon," he'd say when he came to work every day. I read in his obituary from the *Sumter County Journal* in York, Alabama, that the Ku Klux Klan marched around his grave and placed a wreath.

I was embarrassed when I found the obituary. I'd known my ancestors to be drunks, but I'd never known one to be a Klansman. I felt like he had eaten sour grapes, and I was the one whose teeth were on edge.

I think everybody down South feels that way at one time or another. The ones who stop talking long enough to look and listen to the things around them.

Nathan Bedford Forrest, blissfully unaware of how ridiculous he looked in a white sheet, left to us in his will a house they turned into a memorial, then turned into a Walmart when the protesters protested. And he left a golden bowl of sour grapes, with instructions to preserve his work and eat of those disgusting grapes three times a day. He doesn't need his white sheet to appear as a ghost anymore; he comes to breakfast, lunch, and supper every day to spoon-feed those sour grapes into our mouths, like a mother who ought to have her kids taken away.

Edgar Killen died several years ago, in prison where he belonged. They spent fifty years trying to lock him up—trying to lock someone up—for those three murdered young men: civil rights activists. To some, it still sounds like such a strange phrase in the South, "civil rights activists," and I hate that it sounds strange: three men like three moon rocks that fell to Mississippi from high above, landing at the feet of cavemen. Their names were James Chaney, Andrew Goodman, and Michael Schwerner—all under the age of twenty-five. It seems unfair, those three boys cut down in 1964, and Edgar Killen walking free forty years, and only serving thirteen out of sixty—a pretty easy deal if you ask me—before Death granted him that Back Door Parole. I hear he repented in prison and left his land to a Black man. I'm glad if it's true, but I tell you the gruel Edgar Killen ate in the prison commissary every day was like steak and eggs compared to the sour grapes he left each of us, his great-grandchildren, adopted against our will.

"Repentance," they mutter up North. "It's the evangelicals' talk. I hope he rots in hell. Even though there is no hell," they say. "That's more evangelical talk." I don't know what an evangelical is, but I read an old English rhyme somewhere once that said, "Twixt the stirrup and the ground, Mercy I ask'd and mercy I found."

I hope it's true. I hope it's true that Edgar Killen, once a proud member of the Ku Klux Klan—the notorious pack of cowardly wolves in stupid outfits—I hope it's true he repented, truly repented, and I hope he's in heaven right now. And you want to know something else? I hope Governor George Wallace is right beside him, cleansed of his sins, too. Both of those men, one high, one low, both free from the snares of the Fall and the Curse, free of hate, free of their wheelchairs, washed in the Blood of Jesus.

I hope it's so. I hope it's so, if only to make those Pharisees up North twitch with rage.

"Our fathers have eaten sour grapes," those in Judah said, "and the children's teeth are set on edge."

"No," said God Almighty, "your proverb is a lie. Each one shall die for his own sins."

I'm done eating sour grapes fed to me by people I never knew. Let them eat their own deeds. They're my ancestors and would have been my superiors in another time. But it's today, and they're not my people. They don't belong to me. Edmund Ruffin belongs to the aristocrats who told him it was his war to fight. Jubal Early belongs to Robert E. Lee. James Earl Ray belongs to the grave. Strom Thurmond belongs to the Stone Age.

We are harlots in a house of Pharisees. We are told how wretched we are, how our sins are so great they could never be removed, that the mullet and the Lynyrd Skynyrd sticker on the window are a scarlet *A* we're bound to wear forever and ever, to show everyone who comes to this beautiful land what manner of sinners we are.

We weep at Jesus's feet, and the Pharisees muse, "If only this

Man knew what manner of harlots and hillbillies these are who kneel before Him."

I hope whoever told Governor Wallace he could leave behind his sins, leave them at the Cross, is still out there, weeping at the pulpit, making even the most pious of the congregation wriggle in discomfort as he tells the story of the Man who walked on the water to snatch him from the depths. I hope the cherub-faced, dirty Baptist boys who go to Mexico every summer to build a house for the needy are singing "I Saw That Great Judgment Morning" in their church van as it chugs down I-35. Christian soldiers marching as to war, and all that Sunday school stuff. And I hope when they sing it, they remember all the verses about fire and brimstone, and the great men whose greatness could not save them.

I hope the Calvinists and the Anglicans who want to impress the progressives by cleaning up the litter cut down every rotten tree that was ever used as an implement of hell to hang strange fruit. I hope they burn those rotted trees and plant Southern Magnolias and anything on which Spanish moss will droop.

Let us become a ruckus again, the sweetest ruckus ever made; everything in our path will be blessed. We'll make a joyful noise in the house of Pharisees.

Come, it's Sunday: let us cross the river and rest in the shade of the trees.

CAROLYN GUINZIO

Photograph Not Taken

Magnet fishing, the boys
caught an iron wedge.

Its empty bolt holes
spoke of holding some-

thing up—a bridge—
rivets rattling out

under the endless
diesel pickups picking

their way to the good
spots. The boys brought

the wedge home, where,
on the porch table, it held

things down instead.
The trees were bare.

When the sun was low,
through the hole in its side

came a beam that made
a perfect circle of light

on the rusted floor
of what looked, then,

like a tomb of the buried
alive. I meant to lean near

to it, I meant to look closely,
train the lens, hold it in my

eye, the aura cast on a thing
beyond the reach of memory.

I meant to, but by then,
it was gone with the trash.

I thought there would be
more time. I thought I would

have time, but oblivion
quickly took it back

and it's gone:
the one perfect thing

the broken and lost
could still make.

Lumen

You said sorrow is looking in
at the light from outside—

framed in the window, chipped
paint frame, dirt and dead May-

flies and flies, silver threads
of legs left behind by Daddy-

Long-Legs when the frame
came down in Fall, cotton-

ball cocoons abandoned or
defunct, shriveled husks

curled inside, still trying
to hold themselves in. Still

trying to hold the walls
around her, a woman framed

in the squares of light moves
through them, getting ready

for the end. She is tired, and
she longs for the bed. From

outside, it looks like she leaves
things to their disintegration.

Without, you watch over her
under a dome of flickering stars.

The Spoken World

When you run
past the privacy
fence, a story
flickers through
the slats, a flip
book told in real
time: That party
in the yard
went deep
into night.
How far
in the future
seemed
the corpses
of morning:
hard paper fire-
cracker husks,
aluminum,
moths lost
in citronella
wax, fluttered
into oblivion
like tar-pit pigeons.
The kid sits
in a cell of grass,

tasting clover
leaves between
his tiny front
top and bottom
teeth. He holds
his oversized eye
to the sharp hole
of an abandoned
can in which ash
has dissolved
into beer. This
is living. This
is the life.

Plaster Madonna

A WEEK AFTER THE FIRE, Paul lurked through the ruins of the farmhouse with a black garbage bag to collect any objects of memory. In the kitchen, where he'd dragged his mother's body from the flames, the table bowed on three legs toward the window. Dishes had spilled in shattered heaps from the scorched cabinets. He scraped plate shards from the bubbled countertop until he found a small statue of the Virgin Mary, mostly intact, and perched it on the windowsill. He peered into her face.

"Virgin of virgins, Mary Our Mother," he said. Her plaster pupils surveyed the soot-blackened ceiling, sagging from the work of the firefighters' hoses. A spiderweb of fractures ringed the base of the Virgin's neck. Paul swigged from a flask of vodka, then spit on his thumb and rubbed soot from the statue's cracks. Yellow glue like a scarf around her throat revealed previous reconciliations of her head to her body. "How many times did we knock off your head?" he said.

He was nine, the first time he remembered. He and his older brother, Mike, a stuttering fourteen-year-old, were clearing the dinner table. Their parents had gone out to the dairy barn for the evening milking.

"D-do the d-d-dishes," Mike said.

"D-d-do w-w-what, d-d-dummy?" Paul replied.

Mike shoved Paul to the floor and clamped his elbows to the linoleum. He began hammering his sternum with a knuckle. Then Mike hawked up phlegm and dribbled a globule between his lips, the pendulum of mucus spinning thinner with each movement, arcing and swinging, and dropped it into Paul's open mouth. Paul gasped as the spit plopped heavily down the back of his throat, the milky phlegm sucking straight down his windpipe. Mike howled and got up.

Paul rose, coughing, and attacked his brother, aiming to kill him. They lurched into the countertop and clipped the statue. The Virgin's head popped off when she hit the Formica counter.

"L-l-l-look what you d-d-did," said Mike.

Paul's knees buckled at the sight of the decapitated icon, and his cheeks burned. Tears welled, and the kitchen blurred. He caught himself against the kitchen table where his hand happened onto a fork. He gripped it and swung, missing Mike over and over. There was no thought in any of this, simply the target for his anger. Paul squared his feet and hurled the fork, which sliced past Mike's ear and stuck in the wall next to the window. They stared at the resonating fork.

Mike departed wordlessly, leaving Paul to pull the fork out of the wall and clean up the broken saint. In their father John's workshop, Paul found wood glue, and he reset the broken Virgin's head, hailing her mercy. He promised that he would become a priest if she forgave him his rage. At the workbench, he also found his father's bottle of homemade peach brandy. He'd tasted it before when John pulled it from the still, but it had burned then and it felt like a trick his father played on him. This time, he took a large swallow without even trying to taste it, and then pursed his lips.

It burned in his throat like a belch with barbs, but he determined to keep his mouth shut. The fire bloomed in his cheeks and tears dripped from his eyes. The alcohol leaked into his blood and then each of his limbs and fingers called out, but he would not open his mouth. The impotence he'd felt fighting his brother, and the rage that led him to attempt murder weren't emotions for which he had words. He didn't understand how he lost control, or the shame that came with it. But this heat, a flagellation of his cells, became a shape for that feeling, and it was something that could be contained inside his skin.

When the glue dried, he returned the poorly restored Mary to her perch in the kitchen window, but each evening for a month he worried that his parents would notice her broken neck as the family gathered around with rosary beads. Chanting their prayers to the saint: *Remember, O most gracious Virgin Mary, that no one who has sought thine intercession was left unaided . . .*

They never noticed though—or at least never mentioned it. Mike never brought it up. Paul was too afraid to confess. Left unacknowledged, his guilt turned to dread and fermented in his chest. He felt it expand like a trapped vapor with no release.

Now forty years later, in the burned house, he dug a thumbnail into the charred window frame. Ash swirled and stung his throat. He held his breath and finished the prayer from memory: *I fly unto thee, O Virgin of virgins, my mother; to thee do I come, before thee I stand, sinful and sorrowful . . .*

He found the four holes where the fork had stuck and touched the punctures. Three styles of wallpaper had been hung over these holes since he'd thrown the fork, and each layer burned and peeled away in the fire. His hand fell from the wall, and he touched the statue's face. He gripped her around the body like a bottle of wine, or like a bell, and left the ruined house and drove west through the pasture toward his own home. Cattle bearing his brother's brand trotted up to the car. The brand was an M with a P like a flag waving from the M's leg. At one time, the brothers had shared the brand, but Mike had forced him out of the partnership. There hadn't been an argument because Mike didn't like to talk: only an accumulation of unspoken and therefore unmet expectations, and then it was over. It took Paul by surprise, and he was powerless to change Mike's mind. When he attempted to reason with him, Mike brought up Paul's drinking.

"You drink as much as I do," Paul said.

"Not l-l-like you do," Mike replied.

So Mike bought him out and kept the brand.

* * *

Cattle crowded around him as he unhooked the gate that separated their properties.

"I don't have any hay," he said. He held out his hand and one of the red Limousin heifers stretched her neck and sniffed him, and he touched the top of her nose until she allowed him to sidle to her. He patted her neck. "You're a beauty," he whispered into her ear. "Mike's doing something right."

He drained his flask, tonguing the last drop, and stumbled into his car. Leaving the gate unlatched behind him, he drove down the farm-to-market road to his house, ready to settle in for the night.

His wife, Louise, was not home when he opened the front door. He fished around his memory to remember where she said she'd be, but their last conversation had slipped. He set to work measuring coffee into the filter.

He leaned over the sink and scanned east across the plains, finding the burnt house two miles away on the horizon. The elm trees that surrounded the house had burned to spindly stumps. His father planted those trees in 1942 before he was drafted.

Now in this autumn light, the charred trees seemed to Paul as the slag droplets showering from the lightning of his father's welder, splattering and cooling into tiny black branches. Paul filled his sink with soapy water and scrubbed the statue of the Virgin Mary and wrapped her in a towel to dry.

His coffeemaker gurgled and steamed the last drops of hard

water in the machine. From the cupboard, he retrieved a white mug with a chipped rim, the only surviving member of the dish settings he and his wife had received for their wedding. He sought this cup over other cups, running a finger around the various rims until he found the chipped ceramic.

He filled it halfway with coffee, then reached under the sink behind the basket of cleaning supplies for an unlabeled spray bottle, a third filled with a clear liquid. He unscrewed the spray mechanism and filled his mug to the brim, then slurped as much of the hot coffee as he could stand. He held his breath as the alcohol seeped into his chest. His exhale then described the currents of steam over the coffee-warmed spirits.

At the table, he unwrapped the icon. A single piece of white plaster. Hair as white as skin as white as robes. He thumbed the yellow crack in her neck and tried to decipher the turn of her lips. The ambiguity of her smile dislodged a memory.

* * *

He was five. He sat in the front pew of St. Mary's Catholic Church, the parish in which he'd been baptized, gazing at a mural of Mary above the altar. He was alone in the sanctuary, waiting on his father, who was in confession. Tiny cherubim—round-cheeked and locks curled—lifted Mary into heaven. Her white robes swathed in the gold of the surrounding sky. A gold scarf and pink belt, a blue sash billowing like sheets on the line. Lips like rose petals. Her hand extended into the sanctuary beckoning Paul, and her blue eyes regarded the ceiling, so he craned his neck to see her view, and he found a fracture in the ceiling plaster. Was it joy with which she watched the crack? Or worry? Or doubt? Would the crack suddenly grow and ruin the ceiling down on his head? Or did she expect heaven to descend through the break and accommodate the boy in this pew? He grew frightened of either outcome and jumped from his seat to search for his father in the confessional booth.

John's voice leaked through the wicker-pleated dividers, his father speaking in the confessional like he spoke in the shop, as if his words were meted cuts in steel used in the manufacture of a larger implement.

"I killed a boy," said his father. "In Italy. One of ours. His guts were out. Nobody could fix that. He would've died in a few minutes. But he was screaming and Nazis were crawling in the rocks. I needed to hide. I put my hands over his face until I couldn't feel his breath."

"In war . . . " began the priest.

* * *

Paul placed St. Mary on his kitchen table. "Why am I remembering this now?" he asked her, then took another drink and filled the cup again from the cleaning bottle. He covered his eyes and tried to remember what the priest had prescribed for penance, but the memory ended at his father's confession. His hand trembled in the handle of the mug.

At 8:40, after half an hour of drinking at the table, he heard his wife open the back door. He quickly screwed the top back on the spray bottle. Without acknowledging him, she swung open the cupboard. The cups clinked as she chose one. Her gray hair was bound into a ponytail that hung down her back. She didn't turn to face him.

"Where were you?" he asked.

"I told you I was going to help Roxanne put up cowpeas."

"You told me? When?" His tone wasn't as tactful as he had hoped, and she faced him now.

"You were at the desk, looking at your mom's bank files."

"You can't expect me to remember that."

"I don't expect you to remember much anymore," she said.

He saw her eyeing the spray bottle.

"Were you cleaning?" she asked.

"The coffeemaker is backed up. I wanted to run some vinegar through after we finish that pot." He shook the bottle. "But it's empty."

He looked at the clock: 8:45. She poured her cup in the sink without having taken a drink and left the kitchen. Her bedroom door rattled on the other side of the house while he looked out the window.

* * *

Paul had decided to marry Louise when they were seventeen, on the night they snuck wine into a drive-in to see Cool Hand Luke. By the time Lucille the Blonde washed her car and taunted the prisoners, Louise was lying down across the bench seat, and they had to stop to move the gear shift out of the way. His head was fuzzy from the wine, and his focus lagged between senses. Taste mingled with smell in their heavy breathing. Fingers felt inadequate for touch. Her body flickered a pale blue as the projector illuminated the windshield, and the movie manipulated her expressions. Was she ecstatic or angry or in pain?

Afterward, he didn't know what to say. They buttoned their clothes, though they had only been half-undressed, and he held her. They began to sober up as Paul Newman played a song on the banjo. He didn't understand what was happening in the movie, but he knew it was sad. Louise wiped a tear.

"What happened?" he asked.

"That was my first time."

Paul Newman cried and played the song faster. *Get yourself a sweet Madonna . . . .*

"I'd put you on a pedestal, my sweet Madonna," he said. She turned to him, incredulously. He suddenly understood what she meant by her first time. "Oh," he said, "It was mine, too." They decided to leave the movie when the prison guard put Luke in the box again.

He whistled the song as he drove home along the farm-to-market roads. Twenty minutes after he'd dropped off Louise, he could still smell her in his clothes. He breathed deep the scent, thinking he'd marry her and that he'd tell his parents when he got home.

* * *

His mother sat at the kitchen table in her nightgown with a glass of peach brandy.

"Grab another glass," she said.

He slid the glass to her, and she tipped a dram of her brandy into his.

"This batch is good," he said.

"It was a good year for peaches."

"Why are you up?"

"Waiting on you," she said.

"You worried I'm dead somewhere?"

"I'm your mother. I worry about your whole life. All of it."

"I'm alive. You can stop worrying."

She thumbed a drip from the side of her glass and touched her tongue. "Do you know how my father met my stepmother?"

"She was a mail order bride from Schulenberg."

"There's more than that," she said. "My mother died."

"From gangrene, I know. She had a Caesarean when Uncle Harvey was born."

"Yes. Papa had five kids and no wife. I was seven, the oldest."

He sipped his brandy and nodded. She continued. "Us kids all got chores to keep the farm running. Little Eddie would get the eggs. Had to carry a stick to hit the rooster with."

"What was your job?"

"One of my jobs was to tend the corn mash."

"When you were seven?"

"It only had to be kept warm and stirred. It wasn't hard."

"Is that how you learned to make brandy?"

"Everybody could make spirits back then. No one looked down on it. Just another part of a farm. When Prohibition passed, Papa distilled twenty or thirty gallons a week. Too much, probably. The law came around. But he had five kids that he couldn't take into the field while he plowed, so he stayed close to the house to make moonshine.

"In August of '27, I was feeding leftover mash to the chickens, and the sheriff stopped by. I didn't see him, so I couldn't ring the dinner bell as a warning. He wanted a cut of the proceeds. But he told the papers he was doing the work of God and Calvin Coolidge. He arrested Papa right there, with Harvey in diapers, the rest of us crying."

"Papa went to jail? I didn't know that."

"Not jail. He went to prison. Huntsville, five hundred miles from here. The Batenhorsts took us in for six months."

"How'd he get out?" Paul asked, sipping.

"He got his case in front of the governor. Ma Ferguson pardoned him."

"They pardoned him for making moonshine?"

"For selling it. When he got out, he had no way to get back up here, but his sister lived in Schulenberg, which was a couple of hours from Huntsville. He stayed with them for a few weeks, and when he came home I had a stepmother."

"Where'd they meet?"

"Church. They knew each other for two weeks. You can love anyone. Papa was not an easy man, but she loved him. And she was a good mother to us."

"Did you stay awake to tell me this story?" he asked.

"You can love anyone."

"I do love someone."

"You feel a lot for this girl?"

"Louise."

"What?"

"Her name is Louise. And I want to marry her." He drank the rest of the glass and allowed the heat to bring pain. Then he filled the glass again.

She tapped her fingernails on her tumbler. Her fingers were crooked from years of milking cows and quilting.

She glanced at the statue of Mary on the windowsill, and he followed her eyes.

"When did you break the Virgin?"

He tried to appear shocked, but he knew he was caught.

"When I was nine."

"When you were nine?" she said. "When you wanted to be a priest?"

He glanced at the statue of Mary.

"I was nine. I said some things I didn't mean."

"You lied?"

"I didn't know what being a priest would mean. Who holds a nine-year-old to his word?"

"But you're seventeen. Do you know now what it means to keep your word, to vow?"

"Did you know, when you were twenty-one? Dad asked you to be his wife before he left for the war. What did y'all know?"

"We knew what it meant to say something and mean it." She drank the rest of her brandy in a swig. "You can love anyone, now," she said. "In the future, then you can only love one person." She slid the empty glass over to him.

* * *

He tapped his chipped coffee mug with his wedding ring. "Now you know," he said to the memory. "Now you know. Not then." The vodka's legs descended in the empty cleaning bottle. He heard Louise hanging clothes in her closet. The clock's second hand rounded the six.

8:47.

He stood and gulped the entire cup, swooning at the apex, and set the mug down, catching half its base on the table. It tipped, and he swiped and caught the handle. The cup skittered across the table and disappeared over the edge. The sound of breaking porcelain took his breath. He fled the house to his car.

A dull layer of gray floated like dregs on the horizon as he careened onto the farm-to-market highway. Darkness had fallen, and the white line on the shoulder shimmered as if beneath waters— refusing to focus, falling from his view. "*Going ninety, I ain't scary, 'cuz I got . . . ,*" he sang.

He rubbed his eyes and still the highway retreated, so he shook his head and blinked his eyes hard and when he opened them, there stood a red Limousin heifer in the road. The noise engulfed him: safety glass blasted into a plastic suspension, sheet metal crushed and ripped at joints, an open-door warning tone chimed. The engine continued to run.

The heifer bawled at 8:51.

The door was jammed. He pushed against it with his shoulder. The metal creaked. He leaned over the center console, kicked at the door, and it moved enough that he could squeeze through. Once out, he yanked on the door until the hinges bent open. The cow lay on the crumpled hood, lowing. He walked around her and discovered her ruptured belly, and her mangled legs. He glanced toward the lighted sign at Vince's Liquor, half a mile away.

In the trunk, he found a tire iron and tested the weight in his hand and stumbled back to the cow. Slobber and blood strung from her mouth as he set the iron between her eyes. He pummeled her in the forehead and the tool rang in his hand, but the cow didn't flinch, only kept breathing. He swung again. This time the cow screamed a long syllable that broke into an ass-like bray and trembled in his chest. The bellowing continued and he covered his ears, but he could not escape the liquid, gasping screams, so he screamed back at her to die and swung the iron again and again without effect. She continued breathing.

He fled to the trunk and uncovered a box of black garbage bags tucked behind the wheel well, then shook one out and held it next to her head and spit. Then, sliding the bag over her bawling face, he pulled it tight and hugged her around the neck, his hands around her windpipe. The muscles and cartilage clambered against his fingers as she screamed in the bag, but the sounds became quieter and then ended and the breathing, too, finally stopped.

When she finished trembling, he realized the hoarseness of his voice as he'd screamed with her; he realized the tack of her blood coating his hands, his fingers, and he shook them violently—six, seven times until he could no longer hear the splatter on the road and wiped more blood on his jeans. Then he grabbed her tail and pried, but the busted hood held her like a cup.

"Could I burn you?" he asked. "No, that's stupid," he answered.

He kicked the collapsed bumper and hunched over to catch his breath, the alcohol stuck between his stomach and lungs with the familiar barbs. When he stood, he considered the cow still lodged on his idling vehicle and the half mile to the store. A taste emerged on his tongue, a dry paste of thirst.

"What in God's name are you doing, Paul?" he asked. The film of blood, sticky in the grain of his hands, reflected pink in the single headlight. More blood and cud plopped from the heifer's torn stomachs at his feet. The front end of the car drooped under the weight of the carcass.

He returned to the driver's seat and slid the gearshift into drive; the car blundered forward and he smiled at the cobweb of a windshield. Then the remaining headlight flickered and died. He attempted the electric window, but the motor only whined. He stepped out and searched for the light at the store and pulled his hair. He noticed a change in the air: humidity, a storm springing up in the night. The breeze came from the east like a ghost's breath on his follicles. Lightning spoke by sign between the clouds. At his feet, a noise like a stream. Over the clicking of the engine, he heard water running in the bar ditch.

The county dredged these ditches eight feet deep to channel irrigation water away from the road. He got in the car, left the door open, and inched over to the ditch until the nose of the car began to plunge down the decline, and he slammed the brakes. The carcass heaved but settled back onto the hood. He backed up and tried again with more speed. The steering wheel jerked when the front tires dug into the ditchwall and the heifer tipped and slid off. She disappeared into the kochia weeds. He backed onto the road and found the store's light as it winked out, leaving him alone on the dark highway in a flickering favor of dashboard light. "Go home and drink water," he said.

Weaving from ditch to ditch, he reversed the half mile back to his house and left the car in the driveway. The first drops of rain fell on him as he stole back inside. In the kitchen, he washed his hands and swept the pieces of the mug, attempting to piece together the larger shards in the dust pan, but realized most of the remains were simply dust, so he dumped them in the trash under the sink.

He looked out the window in the direction of the house in which he'd been raised but which no longer existed. The glass reflected his kitchen lights, and he found himself in the gaze of Mary Our Mother, standing behind her, and before her in the glass, the night uncoiling in the flashing light of the late rains. The remains of his childhood house silhouetted in the lightning as if light were pouring through the bead.

His wife entered the frame of glass. He lifted the statue in salutation, and he turned to face her.

"I broke her," he said. "When I was a kid. I was angry."

"Where'd you go?" she asked.

He motioned her to follow him to the empty troves around the house: the top, unused cabinet in his bathroom; the crawl space under the closet; a freezer bag of clear slush behind a box of frozen corndogs. "I hide vodka," he said. "I ran out tonight, and I went to get more."

"Why are you telling me this?" she asked.

"I want. I want to stop drinking."

"I've been telling you that for a long time."

He took a deep breath and stuttered that he loved her. "N-now," he said. "I love you now. I'm so angry. I've always been so angry."

"I might leave tomorrow," she said.

He breathed in.

Their silence extended like an exhale compressing more and more deeply until the breather grows dizzy. The lightbulbs incandesced across her countenance, her face framed in graying hair like a veil pulled back, revealing her pale mouth.

DEWAYNE KEIRN

Homecoming Soliloquy

I travel high and far into these rugged hills
until I come to a town that's lost five grocery stores
and a school that had a WPA-built gym. Yet the town
remains with a hundred residents and only a few
are too lazy to breathe. Progress has struck here,
for you can go to Walmart at one score and five miles
convenience, and the schools there are large and modern.
But here the old home is like the town, forlorn and haunted.
The corrugated metal roof leaks can be tarred, the brush cut,
a garden planted and paths formed anew through woods.
I wonder though, where's the cheer without what was?
Even frogs no longer boom in the night like a ship's
foghorn. Some say those frogs didn't survive the ozone's
thinning, that ultraviolet light destroyed their spawn.
But whippoorwills still call sharp and plangent from hedgerows.
Should I imitate them and sit in a rocking chair on a
safer portion of rotted porch and shout greetings
to passersby? Or read a book on positive thinking?
In the town cemetery an Indian of which nothing is known
lies entombed above ground in lichen-ravaged rock slabs,
solitary among tombstones, alone among strangers.
When the willful Ozark wind blows swiftly through
dark cracks between the rocks, a bitter chant emerges.
Beguiled by hope I could sing in antithesis,
deep and base and booming like a frog.

Two Displays (Civil War Battlefield)

Except for men dying on the left and right
of me during the night from incoming
artillery fire, not much happened.

There was no chewing the fat.

We didn't hit the sack.

No breeze stirred stronger than a breath.

Not a single owl gave a hoot.

Except for men dying on the left and right
through the night, not much happened,
though fireflies flickered magnificently
in a display of insect life.

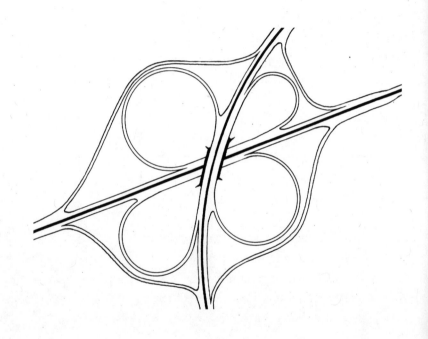

Y'all

1969: Little Rock, Arkansas

I claim *y'all* as my first word, after "mommy" and "daddy." I can't remember a time when this informal second-person pronoun wasn't part of my vocabulary.

1975: Camden, Arkansas

In this little river city an hour north of the Louisiana border, I uttered *y'all* with the same intimacy and comfort I felt while sitting in my mom's lap to watch Sonny and Cher on Sunday nights. *Y'all* exuded the fragrance of the line of pine trees that bordered our small house. Playing in the front yard, I said *y'all* to flora and fauna, like monarch butterflies and the thick white petals of magnolia blossoms. Next door, at Suzy and Cheryl's house, I said, "Do y'all want to play?" Cheryl always did, but Suzy only sometimes.

When I was little, living in Arkansas, Tennessee, and Texas, *y'all* was the pronoun of comfort and belonging, of secrets and fun. Informal and intimate, *y'all* never appeared on the chalk board or in the spelling book.

My brother Chad was born in 1975. The two of us became *y'all*, as in "It's *y'all's* bedtime," or "*Y'all* get ready for church." Chad and I were the children of the family. He and I were *y'all* and *we*, depending on who was speaking. Both *y'all* and *we* connote belonging. With Chad, I belonged to a sibling group, and every time we moved to a new town, we had each other to belong to. He knew what it was like to lose *y'all*.

My dad moved us to Oklahoma so he could get his Doctor of Ministry. His other career interest was teaching, and if he'd chosen that, we wouldn't have moved around so much. I lived in Oklahoma, too, but we didn't say *y'all* there.

2021: Macomb, Illinois

I spend my days alone, so I don't have much use for a second-person plural pronoun—not much opportunity to say to my students: "What do y'all think about bell hooks's article?" or to gossip with my colleagues: "Y'all heard the provost is leaving?" I'm living in the midst of a pandemic, but that's not the reason I'm alone. The reason is that I was laid off from my tenured position in Women's Studies, so I no longer have students or colleagues to address in the second-person plural.

For twelve years, I taught at that state university in Macomb, an island in the middle of industrial corn and soy. In late summer, tall corn stalks send moisture into the air, making it feel even hotter than it is. After harvest, the fields turn dry and dark. "Scorched earth" is the phrase that passes through my mind every time I see them.

This region has two nicknames: Flyover and Forgotonnia. Laid off, I feel flown over and forgotten. They took my *y'all*.

1976: Okeene, Oklahoma

The summer I turned seven, my family moved from Camden, Arkansas, to Okeene, Oklahoma, a prairie town famous for hosting the oldest rattlesnake festival in the world. I started second grade, and that's when I learned about "you guys." We were on the playground, an expanse of flat dirt, and I hoped the other kids would invite me into their game. When they didn't, I said, "Hey, y'all."

A girl named Carmen crinkled her freckled nose at me. "Yaaaaall," she said, as if it were verbal vomit.

"How do you say it, then?"

"You guys," she said. "You. Guys."

They didn't invite me to play. Standing there in the dirt by myself, I felt exposed and inadequate, like I didn't matter. That was an experience of censorship and silencing: *Don't say "y'all." If I say "y'all," I'll be rejected.*

Before the interaction with Carmen, it had been bad enough that I'd missed Arkansas, where my friends, like Suzy and Cheryl, spoke like I did. In Okeene, facing the rattlesnake-ridden plains of humiliation and rejection, I abandoned *y'all* for "you guys." After that, I didn't take language for granted.

1979: Humboldt, Tennessee

The summer I turned ten, we moved east along the Bible Belt, to Humboldt, Tennessee. Humboldt was dissected by railroad tracks. My mom said that White people lived on one side, and Black people on the other, which was mostly true, but we all attended the same school. The segregation of neighborhoods would explain why I hardly saw Black people outside of school.

Also, Humboldt hosted a Strawberry Festival every year and they served giant strawberry pie.

At the Central Avenue Christian Church, where my dad was the new minister, Nate Nunn heard me say "you guys." He contorted his arched nose in disgust and mocked me. Nate was good-looking, and I wanted him to like me, so I switched back to *y'all*. It was easy, like restoring my default settings, but I had become self-conscious, and *y'all* didn't feel as cozy as before. I uttered *y'all* with my taste buds: it was like leftover mashed potatoes and canned gravy, cold and congealed. Later, when I made friends, *y'all* recovered some of its warmth.

1982: Humboldt Junior High School

In the hallway between classes, a tall boy with wiry black hair grabbed my crotch as if it were a can to kick hard and far. It didn't occur to me to tell anyone—not a *you* or a *y'all*, or a *Ma'am* or a *Sir*. No one. Instead, I vomited, for weeks, losing the strength to go to school or practice piano. In the hospital, they dripped fluid into my veins through a needle.

I didn't feel safe. I didn't feel worthy of belonging. I spent more time alone, playing the piano or watching bad TV. I exiled myself from *y'all*.

1984–1987: Houston, Texas

The summer I turned fifteen, we moved down to Houston, a sprawling modern city where everybody said *y'all*. I could speak without anxiety over my second-person plural pronoun, but the thing is, I was withdrawn, hardly speaking to more than one person at a time, and for that, I needed only "you."

By junior year, I quit piano, got my *y'all* back, and became a cheerleader. I believed cheerleading would prove me worthy and keep me safe in school, but the best thing about it was that I got to say *y'all* a lot, and when others said it, they were including me. I belonged.

1987: Macomb, Illinois

My dad took a church here, so we moved again. Inside the little grocery store, near the Wheat Chex, my mom and I sensed an eavesdropper. I'll call her an "accent stalker" because she followed us around the store just to hear how our vowel sounds spread into the air like tupelo honey on Texas toast. When she realized we were on to her, she said something like this: "Excuse me. I love the way you talk. It's so unusual. Where are you from?"

"Arkansas, Oklahoma, Tennessee, and Texas." I pronounced those thirteen syllables with pride, for I had survived those little Bible Belt towns and that sprawling city near the Gulf Coast, and I had an accent to prove it.

Macomb's courthouse square is famous for hosting a speech by Abraham Lincoln. Obama, too, spoke on our square. The courthouse is red and has a white clock tower. That's where I met T, who has never made fun of my second-person pronoun. We attended the university together.

At the university, I learned about the tenure system—how it was created to protect academic freedoms, and I believed this was wonderful—that in the United States, we so valued free speech and the dissemination of critical and creative thought, that we'd developed a system to protect professors. After feeling silenced most of my life for something as small as my second-person plural pronoun, and as big as the sexual assault I sustained, I was drawn to the idea of tenure. I fantasized that *tenure* and *y'all* overlapped in meaning; both connoted security and belonging.

2021. Macomb, Illinois

I go down to the basement to get a box of old newspapers. T had saved the editions of *The Courier* that contained pieces I'd written as a student. Now the papers are brittle and yellowed. I had written an op-ed entitled "Y'all Just Don't Understand Accents," dated October 22, 1988. In the headshot next to my column, my bangs are flying high, half-curled and half-teased, like Madonna's. I still spent a lot of time on hair and makeup. I guess you can take the belle out of the South, but it's harder to take the South out of the belle.

In the op-ed, I wrote that the only time in my life I could "talk in peace," meaning without anyone mocking me or drawing misguided conclusions, was when I was a young child, living in southern Arkansas. To the Arkansan ear, my speech was pure and perfect.

1995: Mount Vernon, New York

For graduate school, I traveled to the East Coast. At a party, where everyone wore very dark charcoal sweaters, a woman heard me talking, and I probably said "y'all," as I often did. The woman said, "Are you from the South? I love Southern culture. Do you like Flannery O'Connor?"

"I guess." I lied, not remembering if I'd read O'Connor in school.

Y'all—that word that had been to me as mundane as leftovers, that word I was ostracized for on the playground, that word I had to unlearn and relearn—now *y'all* was as lauded as a Flannery O'Connor short story.

1997: Macomb, Illinois

My brother drowned in the Spoon River at the Bernadotte dam, forty-five minutes from Macomb. Melting snow had made the river rush, and the current pulled their canoe over the dam and sucked them under.

T and I were newly married and living in Tarrytown, New York. We flew back. *Y'all* was in the community that crowded every inch of the church, upstairs and down. My relatives came up from Tennessee, Texas, and Missouri. Most of them had moved out of Arkansas.

Y'all was missing from my mother. Grief disabled her, and she couldn't walk without friends propping her up. My brother was trapped underneath the Bernadotte dam, and my mother was a ghost of herself. I was the shadow of a ghost. *Y'all* was everywhere and nowhere.

2010–2015: Macomb, Illinois

I returned to the rural town where I'd been a university student, but this time as a professor with a job of my own. By then, I had become comfortable and confident enough in my teaching to let myself utter *y'all* in the classroom.

We were reading *Letters on the Equality of the Sexes and the Condition of Women* (1838), in which Sarah Grimké decries the fact that in the South, women slaves were forced to act as breeders, as well as kitchen and field laborers.

I noticed one of my students staring at me with a look of discomfort.

"Did I say something wrong or offensive?" I explained to them that, like everyone, I have unconscious bias, and that when talking about race, I make mistakes. I apologized.

"No, Dr. Stovall. It's that you be puttin' on an accent." The student said it with a smile that put me at ease. I know these were her exact words because I wrote them down after class. Was it true that when I talked about the South, my accent rang out on its own, without me noticing?

I told the class I was from Southern Arkansas, and that was just how I talked, and again I wondered if the lilt of my speech, not the meaning I sought to convey, put people off.

2015–2016: Macomb, Illinois

It seemed I was noticing more people saying *y'all*. Was my native second-person pronoun moving north? This might have been a wonderful opportunity to recultivate my mother tongue, if words had been effective during the Illinois state budget showdown.

It was during my tenure year. This should have been a happy time, for I had been working toward this goal for over two decades, and finally I had met criteria. But a new governor starved the university, and the administration then targeted my department for elimination.

Meanwhile, the dean had pushed us out of Currens Hall and sent us up to a spooky corner of Simpkins Hall. The move into a building that was rumored to be haunted—and during economic austerity—unsettled me, jumbling my words.

In class, I said, "I expect *you all* to read and come to class." I stood right there in front of my students, and they looked right back at me, from their tables for two, and I suddenly became aware of the fact that my *y'all* had become "you all." By inserting the "oo" sound and separating it from the "all," I'd dug a fault line, and it felt like my heart was losing its rhythm.

"You" functions as plural on its own, depending on context. "All" is unnecessary. "You all" is a broken form of "y'all." There's a gap between "you" and "all," an empty space, a place for my pain. A teacher has to have students, and I feared I was about to lose mine. If they eliminated my position, would I still be a teacher? What would be left of my life's work? The possibility of losing my identity and my students was so devastating that I pushed it way down inside somewhere, and let the sorrow fill the dark, invisible gap I'd dug between "you" and "all."

Maybe "all" meant something different at that moment. I wanted it all: my students, my classes, my family, my tenure—all of it. And I wanted my self too. If I lost my students, I might lose my identity. Regularly uprooted from home—from Arkansas, Oklahoma, Tennessee, and Texas—I had learned to seek *y'all* other ways, and I believed I'd found it in academia. For decades, I had tied my sense of purpose and self-worth to my career. Without it, I'd be nothing.

I was so overwhelmed by fear, that I forgot how to use *y'all*, the most basic word of my childhood and adolescence. My language was breaking down, and with it, my heart. I had done my part for the university, documenting my commitment with annual portfolios of teaching, research, and service. As women academics are expected to do, I went above and beyond, earning awards from the Western Organization for Women and from UNITY, the student group that advocated for the LGBTQ community. My female colleagues were similarly accomplished. For women in academia, "good enough" is never good enough.

The administration eliminated my department and terminated my contract in 2017. My *y'all* was taken. I haven't recovered it.

2021: Macomb, Illinois

It's not unusual anymore for folks to say *y'all* up here, but it's not the same *y'all* I grew up on. In rural Illinois, *y'all* can have an emphatic function: it's used to preface an important statement, as in, "*Y'all* make sure to vote!" Or it can go on the end of a sentence, for emphasis: "Wear a mask, *y'all*." *Y'all* motivates and empowers. It calls us to wake up and pay attention.

I don't remember *y'all* having such a connotation when I was young. In Arkansas, Tennessee, and Texas, in the '70s and '80s, it was mundane, as in "*Y'all* want barbecue or pizza?" or "*Y'all* stop making me laugh so hard my stomach hurts."

2022: Chicago, Illinois

Y'all, I knocked myself out trying to achieve success, and all that work never convinced me that I belong. Y'all, I've been laid off for five years. The university kept offering my classes but staffed them with people who had no degree in the field. Y'all, two male professors in situations similar to mine got their layoffs rescinded. I applied for other academic positions, y'all, but while I was investing my expertise into that institution, my PhD was aging itself out of a market that prefers new degrees. So now I'm an MFA student in creative writing somewhere new.

My words were falling apart, but I'm putting them together. Someday I'll get my *y'all* back. And it will be the Arkansan *y'all*. It will be reliable and fragrant, like wild blackberry bushes in season, at the end of the block. It will be warm, like sunshine on magnolia blossoms. It will be the *y'all* of belonging and recognition. Already, I hear it emerging, softly, from the roots of the Arkansas pines.

TODD OSBORNE

Belief-Making

—*after Ada Limón with thanks to Jon Riccio*

In OK I always claimed no belief
in cardinal directions—could you tell
me if Perkins is south or west

of Stillwater? Could anyone? There's,
of course, so much people like to say:
the sun rises somewhere and goes to bed

somewhere else: as if that explains
anything. I moved south or west
of Stillwater and then I moved back

into town. I still haven't processed
all of that. It's easy, I think, to believe
the sun will keep rising, based

on prior experience, but harder
to believe that your body will
cease to exist one day: it has just

kept going for so long at this point.
In the morning, I wake up and drive
south or west (definitely: south)

and then I drive home oppositely.
One arm tans in the morning
driving south, in the afternoon

north—or maybe the other way 'round.
Try something true: treat other people
like *your* people, a compass triangulating

or re-triangulating your idea of home.
Let's re-imagine the Wild West, if we can.
No massacres. No stolen land. We'll only

try at the places that claim us, not the other
way 'round. We'll pick a direction—south,
west—we'll make it ours: we'll be made.

Epithalamium for Pandemic Wedding

All spring we make plans only for them to change
before summer: we have a venue, then a smaller
one, and then: there will be people, but all our
friends will watch from home. We arrange
everything with our families, ask them to stay
inside for a few weeks. My parents have birds
to keep them occupied, and there's TV: words
said in a certain order to help us feel okay

or remind us everything isn't. I keep wanting
to talk about love. The past arrives to push
closed each door that reads *sound, image,*
rhyme. We see the room once, light slanting
through the windows, then the room, hushed
and barely occupied, and our marriage

begins. We smile for pictures taken by your
sister, my father. My sister plays pastor
one more time, there are 3 people here who are
not technically family, though they are close
enough to be considered such. It is a day
of joy in the middle of a sea of sadness
that has gotten so deep we cannot touch
its bottom, its current quick and rage-inducing.
I keep wanting to talk about your beautiful
face, or let you know that this poem is, yes,
somehow a love poem. I can write a poem
about anything except my own happiness,
it seems, but I am trying to write into that

as much as I can. We got married in the
afternoon, and then got drinks at a gas station
you frequented as a kid. We got snacks
from Walmart. Hibachi to go. That night
we couldn't sleep, I recited each president
from memory. It didn't help us sleep
any better, but it didn't hurt. I don't like
to romanticize the past (or I only romanticize
the past)

but that was, in spite of everything else
happening in the world, a singular, unblemished day.

LAURIE MARSHALL

Mrs. Breedlow Needs the Number for a Reliable Handyman

A T 2:07 P.M. on a sunny Saturday afternoon, Mitch Breedlow rinsed a smear of low-fat tuna salad off his plate and placed it in the only open spot in the dishwasher. He shook the last of the powdered detergent into the appropriate compartment and closed the door. He wrote "dish det." on the grocery list his wife, Brenda, kept on the refrigerator next to the weekly coupons.

At 2:07 p.m. on October 9th, a 2009 Peterbilt was traveling east on Arkansas Hwy 14 in rural Poinsett County.

Mitch called to his dog, Blue, and opened the front door of his home, a red brick split-level situated under a mature stand of loblolly pines. Mitch and Brenda enjoyed sitting on the front porch in the evenings. They watched cars go by and talked about where they would go if they owned one of those RVs the size of a school bus. Mitch didn't read as much as Brenda, but he thought the sound of the pines when the wind was blowing up high in the branches was something like a poem.

Blue jumped off the recliner, tongue flopped over teeth, and flung himself into the mid-afternoon sunshine. Mitch checked the doorknob to keep from accidentally locking himself outside again. He took ginkgo biloba every morning.

With tires, the total weight of a 2009 Peterbilt wheel is approximately 191 pounds. They are held in place by ten steel bolts attached with a hydraulic torque wrench.

At 2:13 p.m. on the first Saturday he'd had off work in two

months, Mitch stood in his front yard watching Blue wander from tree to tree, searching for the freshest squirrel scent to piss on. He thought he'd go to the garage after Blue finished his business to retrieve a screwdriver and a ladder and get busy repairing the sagging gutter over the porch. Brenda pointed it out two weeks earlier as they worked a crossword one evening on the porch, but he kept forgetting. He rolled up the sleeves on his favorite flannel shirt. He texted his wife, "It's gutter day!"

At 2:15 p.m. on October 9th, one of the right rear wheels of a 2009 Peterbilt traveling east on Arkansas Hwy 14 detached from its trailer and struck Mitch Breedlow, 62, as he stood in his front yard. He was pronounced dead at the scene. The State Police report described conditions at the time of the accident as clear and dry.

Suspicion in Flood Time, 1937

Drought is a burn I've learned, scarring an-d chapped. But flood is a terror
you'll climb any damn thing out of only to starve in the sky.

We hear that tributaries turned Arkansas to sea—they say the Ohio-Mississippi
Valley. My people are Arkansas, don't know Ohio anything. We fled before

the January water could reach the mules' chests. We tried to wait out
the freezing waters, but it seeped through our floorboards, the Saint Francis

River swallowing our whole farm. I kept looking higher: walls, pines, animals.
It wasn't going to stop. It would reach our honeymoon horseshoe over the door—

the lucky lovers kissing. I packed the wishbone from before our firstborn
and my Black Cat Ashes Perfume. *Of all the things*, my husband said.

I said, *Believe me, the rest is accounted for.* The water runs, so we run.
Locking down is to be felled like everything else built or grown up.

Water only runs. We run to a still place. We hear there are lines
for food and beds—a new city of us holed-up where the fair comes in May.

Refugees in a city of bluffs studying the cresting. Paid to do good
never worked except sometimes a preacher's call. If they aren't kin or made family

at a fire, what is there to stay with? We cannot put our lives in the care of
nobody in a uniform. In Memphis, the cross is red. The badge is sharp. No.

Our room will be small for a dozen of us. Food from our pantries and wagons, scarce, but we will know where it comes from. The wrapping's from home.

I can figure other families but not a government nobody separating us, making us into lines and numbers. We can ration our own selves, stay warm on higher ground.

There is no water, rising into more rising. My husband will smile at our horseshoe safe under our bedroll. We will sit down and breakfast together, hungry but dry.

The Poet-Historian Sucks Her Teeth; 2020 Is Not 1811

Uttering *unprecedented* marks you a fool
You forget the year of the biggest flood in three decades
a river channel simply changed   to submerge all
of Napoleon, Arkansas
Pestilence made for stunted crops   then a solar eclipse
where passenger pigeon roosts broke the damn trees
The year millions of gray squirrels tried   to swim across
the Mississippi which was running upstream   a tidal pulse
from the river alligator god's heart   a wet choking
in blood and brown
Finally an earthquake so strong   two months of aftershocks
dropped chunks   of northwest Tennessee twenty feet
Now above a bald cypress forest   is Reelfoot Lake
a field trip favorite
What we know of *today*   comes from catastrophe

After the Levee Breaks Again

Can you call it one wave if it wasn't ocean or God-made?
It crested a freight train whose engine was another fire lost
to Mississippi. Crop, animal, farm. Families climbed the boxcars.
Can you also call the living *what was washed up*?

Memphis, the fourth Chickasaw bluff downstream from Fort Pillow,
is the crossroads of Tennessee, Mississippi, and Arkansas. Hoover stood
on the bank, as baffled as he ever showed anyone. *The Mississippi
is ten times more than Niagara at maximum flood stage.*

Divers throw switches from underneath. Thirty survey planes
cover 400 hundred miles twice per day. WWI vets can aim
a parcel into roof dwellers' hands, but worry is looking at the water
and food about to poison. Tomorrow's forecast is most unkind.

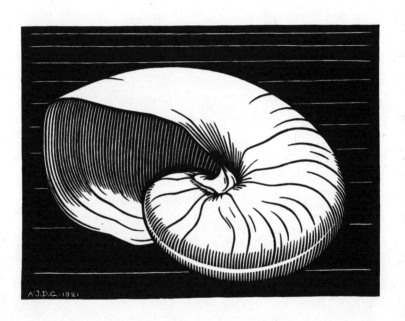

Frog Creek Crow

JUST PAST THE BROKEN CRAWFISH HUT and around the turn of the curve where the splintered bridge crossed Frog Creek Crow—down at the end of the Chavaniac cul-de-sac, the magnolia tree, which was once large and alive and magnificent, had toppled over, broken in half, rotted and bare. Its branches, twigs—remnants—brown and cracked leaves scattered around, littering patches of grass and dirt, making Aristide feel tired. He stood on the front of his porch in his underwear, one hand rubbing his stomach, the other scratching his thigh. It was morning but his forehead had already gathered sweat as the humidity had settled in from the rains the night before.

Behind him, under the creaking ceiling fan, a straw chair—seventeen years old, which he had made when he was just a child, an apprentice of his dad who was a carpenter by trade. A hard-working man, Aristide's father was, playing an important role in his life before he had passed away two years ago in March. Aristide remembered his father as a kind, gentle person—one who avoided arguments by telling stories and through those tales, many lessons Aristide had learned whether it was at the time or later on in his life. Not once could Aristide remember his dad raising his voice or expressing any frustration and anger.

The broken magnolia before him—he remembered sitting with his father on the porch on particularly windy days, watching the thriving magnolia tree lose its flowers, floating and whispering away into the sky.

"They'll come back," his father would say, every time. "Before you know it, they'll be back glittering our tree like it was meant to be."

And he would sip on his iced tea—Aristide, his lemonade—until the mosquitoes came out in full force, which meant it was dinner time. When it rained, his dad would stick out his glass to get one drop of rain.

"Got to love the sky, son," he would say every time.

For dinner—red beans and rice were the staples in their household, and neither Aristide nor his father became tired of it.

"Simple, and to the point, and it gets the job done," his dad would say, laughing. "Much like me, I'd like to think."

Aristide had eventually perfected his dad's red beans and rice.

"It's always in the timing," his dad said. "Everything is in its timing."

It had taken Aristide some time, but through many attempts of tasting and failing, he was able to eventually find the savory tint to his cooking.

The day before his dad died, as they sat on the porch and as the magnolia tree released its bloom into the air, Aristide's father didn't speak or say his usual phrase. He remained quiet. And Aristide remained quiet. And the next morning, just before breakfast, he found his dad dead on the floor, just next to the bed his father and his mother had slept in for years—the certain amount, Aristide didn't know. He didn't know how long they were together. He didn't know how long they were married and for how long they were married before he was born. He didn't know much about his mother.

Early in their marriage, she left them, not giving any explanation, four years after she had given birth to their son. He couldn't remember his mother much—how she looked, the sound of her voice, the clothes she wore—just vague shadows flickered as he tried to remember her. He created images of her and saw long dark hair, watery eyes, tanned skin, wearing a long yellow dress. Her voice—soft and welcoming, and she had a loud laugh. He knew that these memories that he had made for himself were bits and pieces from mothers of his friends or other people he knew.

Aristide's father never talked about Sidonie, but there were times, Aristide could tell, that Avit wanted to, or that he was thinking about her—as at rare times at night, when his father thought he was sleeping, Aristide would be awake listening to his dad cry in the next room. Sometimes, he would see his father looking through old photos—pictures his dad would never show him. Her clothes were still neatly kept in the dresser, and when he fixed the bed in the mornings, he would always puff up her pillow.

As he stood there on the porch, still looking at the snapped magnolia, he thought about the morning Avit died.

"Dad," Aristide said, looking down at him on the floor. He nudged him a few times before turning him over so that he faced the ceiling. His chest wasn't moving. He was wearing his favorite plaid shirt—one, Aristide had assumed, that was a gift from Sidonie. Aristide ran outside of his house and across three fields before reaching the nearest neighbor. When Lilia opened the door, Aristide was out of breath. He leaned over panting.

"What's wrong, honey?" Lilia asked. "Would you like something to drink?"

Just behind her, brushing against her legs was a pup—a chocolate Labrador. As he continued to breathe hard, he looked into the eyes of the dog and felt an unexpected sensation of love.

"Dad," Aristide said.

He shook his head, and Lilia ran to the phone, while Aristide stayed at the front door. He could hear her talking, but it was muffled—the world to Aristide was muffled as he just tilted his head and looked into the watery eyes of the Labrador pup. He reached out his hand, and she licked his fingertips, looking sad.

"So simple," he said.

Lilia rushed back from the kitchen to the front door and in one motion, she swooped up the pup and grabbed Aristide by the arm.

"Come on, Sunshine," she said.

Aristide almost fell as she pulled him by his hand.

"They're coming," she said. "I'll drive you back."

They got into a red truck—Sunshine sat on Aristide's lap. Lilia put down the windows and revved the engine before screeching out of the driveway.

"I just wish," Lilia said. "I just wish that Avit kept a phone at the house—specifically for reasons like this."

Aristide thought about the conversation he had with his dad about how he didn't like using phones, but he only liked to talk to people in person.

"It's the faces, son," he once told Aristide. "The faces tell you every story you need to know."

Aristide gently rubbed the top of Sunshine's head. Lilia lit a cigarette and took two long puffs before throwing it out the window.

"Is he dead, honey?"

"I think so."

"Oh, honey."

Lilia almost ran into the front of their house, just braking at the front of the porch—next to the truck was the majestic magnolia tree. Lilia ran inside, but Aristide remained, whispering to Sunshine as tears came down his face.

There was the burial.

He was buried as requested, between his two dogs, who had passed away before Aristide was born. The hallways of their house were covered in framed photos of the two dogs, and Aristide knew how important it was to his dad to be buried with them.

After the funeral, Aristide took over his dad's business. It wasn't easy for him. Though he had learned much under his dad's mentoring, he knew he lacked both the experience and the confidence to maintain the business as his father had done. Errors in measurements, the wrong supplies, forgotten tools, broken materials, living on his own—these were just some of the obstacles Aristide had faced as he learned the trade.

There were times when he would just sit on his dad's bed and cry, much like Avit had done when he was thinking about Sidonie. There were times he wanted to quit it all and just work at Lilia's restaurant, boiling crawfish and shrimp. It was the magnolia tree that kept him going, knowing how much Avit had loved it—his love for the magnolia and the conversations they had on the porch about the tree were embedded in Aristide's soul, memories that only became stronger as time passed.

The city of Lafayette helped him out—those who lived nearby and those who lived across town, all who had known Avit and had watched Aristide grow up since he was born supported him. Especially when he was young, but even when he was a teenager, Aristide practically lived at various businesses and homes as his father worked at these places, becoming friends with his clients and their children, being fed on-site, and even being scolded when he was in trouble—they were all uncles and aunts to him. Though much work could have been done by the owners themselves—whether it was their own houses or businesses, they wanted to make sure Aristide would be financially secure. Not only that, but they wanted to keep him busy as to not think about the passing of his father—shops, houses, sheds, tractors, gardens and the like gave Aristide purpose during a time when he felt lost. Even other carpenters helped him, suggesting to some of their customers that they should reach out to Aristide instead.

He worked nonstop for two years, nothing but routine—breakfast, work, lunch, work, dinner, sleep. Red beans and rice every day, and every now and then, the local folk would drop by to keep him company. He learned the trade and became a strong carpenter, but as his life settled into normalcy again, and during those nights alone at his home, Aristide struggled with his thoughts.

It didn't surprise him, on one night, how he had contemplated taking his own life though the idea had never entered his mind until that day. As he opened one of the kitchen drawers and took out a knife, then facing the opened window that gave way to the backyard, sprinkled with hibiscuses, azaleas, and irises, he closed his eyes and saw himself in his father's lap. A voice came to him—a voice he felt like he should remember, singing a lullaby that he wasn't sure if he had heard before. The tune made him open his eyes and put the knife back in the drawer, and from that night on, he never slept in his own room or on his father's bed or in the house at all, but in the back patio, on a hammock that stretched from one oak to another—shielded from the sky with a wooden roof Avit had made years ago. But whether he was in the house or outside in the backyard, Aristide didn't get much sleep since the passing of Avit. Long nights awake, red eyes, too tired to shower or cut his fingernails, his way of life had completely transformed into a mode of stagnant numbing sensations where he failed to take care of himself.

Regionally Catholic, still Aristide didn't know much about church and God and praying, and after the night in the kitchen, he set himself on his knees, bedside, clasped his hands and closed his eyes and tried to pray. He tried to pray but he didn't know how to—his words and his thoughts went everywhere except to his intentions.

"What do I do?" he whispered, eyes tightly closed.

He opened them.

"What do I say?"

He left it at that.

So on that morning, Aristide, as he stood there on the porch and looked at the forlorn tree, wondered what his father would've done with it—he wondered what happened, how he, himself, could've let the magnolia fall apart as it did. He was too focused on the business, not noticing the withering magnolia.

"It's my fault," he said.

He lit a cigarette, a habit he had developed only recently, and took in a deep breath.

"I'm sorry, Dad," he said. "I'm so tired. I miss you."

He barely washed up, and it took all of his energy to brush his teeth. Putting on some jeans and his favorite T-shirt—a faded green cloth with a yellow imprint of an owl, gifted to him by Avit—he walked alongside Frog Creek Crow and followed its path to the coulée. It was a quiet morning, and only the melodies of birds and the rushed sounds of squirrels rustling through a line of trees could be heard. He counted how many pieces of trash he passed as he walked. There—at the coulée—as always, was Grinnie, sitting on a patch of grass amid dirt with a fishing rod and a boombox. Don McLean's "American Pie" was playing, and Grinnie was gently singing along. Aristide crouched down next to him and listened. He continued to sing as he patted Aristide on the back, without looking at him. It didn't take too long for Aristide to join his friend, and their voices became louder and louder, smirking and laughing as they sang. When the song came to an end, Grinnie pressed the Stop button and then Rewind, still not saying any words to Aristide—he pressed Play and the song came on again. Aristide looked beyond the coulée where there was a bright green pasture, a few cows grazed—their hooves wet from morning dew.

"This song and only this song, right Grinnie?"

He nodded his head.

"On repeat until I die."

"That should go on your grave."

"It better."

Grinnie lit a cigarette—taking a couple of puffs, he handed it over to Aristide and lit another one.

"You're in charge of that, Aris," he said. "When I go, you get that on my stone, and I'll be happy to be dead."

Aristide exhaled.

"I got you."

A hawk flew overhead—its wings spread wide as Aristide looked at it with one eye closed in the rising sun. It soared away until the blue sky engulfed its flight.

"Do you pray?" Aristide asked.

"What's that?" Grinnie said.

"Like do you pray?"

"What do you mean?"

"Folding your hands and bowing your head and all."

Grinnie puffed on his cigarette and took in a deep breath before exhaling. He spat.

"Yeah I pray. You?"

"I don't think I know how to."

"What do you mean?"

"I tried once, but I didn't know what to do."

Grinnie laughed.

"Just do what you just said—put your hands together and bow your head."

"And then what?"

"That's up to you—pray what you feel like praying for."

Aristide looked at the cows on the other side of the coulée—a calf standing next to its mother, he assumed.

"What do you pray for, Grinnie?"

"I don't know, you know. I just pray."

"Do you pray for me?"

"Sure I do, Aris," he said, patting him on the back.

"When I figure it out, I'm going to pray for you."

"I appreciate that."

Without missing a beat, he started singing along again. Aristide listened to him, in unison with McLean. He admired his friend's voice, and he would always try to get him to play in front of a crowd, but Grinnie kept his talents to himself.

"You can get real big," Aristide once said.

"I want to be small."

When the song finished, Grinnie rewound the tape and played it again.

"You think my mom is still around?" Aristide asked.

"I do, Aris," Grinnie said, as if he had been wondering about it just as much as Aristide.

He hummed along to the song.

"I think I want to find her."

Grinnie put the volume down but not all the way down.

"I wouldn't be surprised if she lived somewhere nearby."

"Really?"

Grinnie spat and nodded his head.

"How do I find her?"

"The library."

"What's that?"

"The library."

"How?" Aristide combed the dirt with his fingers.

"Through the desktop computers."

Grinnie lit another cigarette and gave it to Aristide, who had made a mound out of the dirt. He patted it softly.

"They have desktop computers we can use—you know Charlotte?"

"I know Charlotte," Aristide said.

He thought about her red hair and freckles.

"She can help you out. One time I went to the library, and she helped me find a spark plug on the Internet. I ordered it and everything. Maybe you can look your mom up."

Aristide felt his chest tighten—nervous.

"Maybe it's not a good idea."

Grinnie spat and put his arm around Aristide's shoulder. He hummed for a bit.

"I get it," he said. "But maybe think about it. Or at least you know it's there if you want to look for her."

"You think I should?"

"Sometimes I put myself in your life, especially over the past couple of years, and I think I would do it. I'm not saying that you should do it, but I would—I would want to find her."

The two remained silent and listened to "American Pie" a few more times, chain smoking and watching the cows under the sun.

"I got to get," Grinnie said.

"Yeah."

"Look," Grinnie said.

He pointed down the road and gave him the directions. It was in the part of town that Aristide wasn't too familiar with, but he figured that he could walk it.

"About thirty-five minutes by the way you walk," Grinnie said.

He gave Aristide the rest of his cigarettes and the lighter, and after a hug, Aristide took off for the library. It wasn't so much that Aristide minded the distance of the walk, meaning the physical exertion of it, but it was more the amount of time it gave him to think about Sidonie. He still wasn't sure if he really wanted to find her or search for her. What if she was still around? What if she moved across the country or what if she was already dead? What would you say to her? Would you meet with her—his mind was full of thoughts, those that had never entered before.

"Sidonie," he whispered over and over to himself, hoping that just by saying her name, it would help him to make his decision.

As he went on his way, he waved at every truck driving by and counted every piece of trash he passed—he lost count at times and started over. Sometimes he counted every bird he saw or the dead opossums, armadillos, and squirrels on the road. Occasionally, he was offered a ride—sometimes by acquaintances, other times by strangers, but he declined on both as he wanted to focus on his thoughts.

Aristide was drenched in sweat by the time he arrived at the library—his shirt soaked and his hair wet, he didn't take much notice of it. He was nervous as he walked in and looked around, feeling overwhelmed. There was a line at the front desk, but beyond, he saw a row of computers. The musk of the books caused his allergies to act up—watery eyes, and it didn't take too long for him to sniffle. He sneezed, standing in front of a computer—a tap on his shoulder.

"I've been meaning to get in touch," Charlotte said.

Aristide tucked in his stomach and stood up straight. Seeing Charlotte made him more nervous. He wiped his nose.

"It's been a while," he said.

"I'm so sorry."

"Monkey bars," Aristide said.

They had gone to grade school together—being good friends back then—but when Charlotte changed schools after fifth grade, they hadn't kept in touch. Aristide thought about the playground—a massive castle made of wood. He spent most of his time on the monkey bars, and talking to Charlotte took him back to one particular day during recess. He was swinging on the bars but the blisters on his palms were too painful and he fell, landing on his back—making it hard for him to breathe. Once he was able to open his eyes from the pain, he saw Charlotte's face peering over him.

"Are you bleeding?"

Aristide coughed, trying to breathe.

"Are you hurt?"

Again, he couldn't answer.

"You look hurt."

Aristide lifted his head and then put it back against the ground and took in deep breaths, coughing.

"I don't know," he managed to say.

A bump on the back of his head had already formed—he felt its pressure as his head throbbed.

"Do you want my Fruit Roll-Ups?" Charlotte asked.

Tears came down his face though he wasn't crying.

"We can trade," he said. "I have a Chocolate Swiss Roll."

A small crowd had formed around him, and eventually one of the teachers came and gave the help that he needed.

"I remember that," Charlotte said. "That seems like forever ago."

"It was the best Fruit Roll-Up I ever ate."

"I'm glad you're okay," she said, laughing.

Her mood took a serious tone.

"I'm really sorry," she said. "I really meant to get in touch, but you know, with work and all, and I have two kids—it has been nonstop."

"It's great to see you," Aristide said.

He looked at the computer.

"Do you need some help?" Charlotte asked.

"I do."

He told her.

"Oh," Charlotte said.

She looked down at the carpet.

"Sidonie. This might be the first time I've heard you mention her name."

"She's been on my mind lately."

Charlotte paused, still not looking at Aristide, and sat down in front of the computer, pulling up a chair next to her for Aristide.

She logged in, using her account and as she typed, Aristide looked at her freckles, freckles he hadn't seen in years—it reminded him of home.

Aristide didn't know his mother's maiden name, and they tried a variety of terms in the search engine. *Sidonie. Sidonie Lafayette La. Sidonie Guidry. Sidonie Obituary. Sidonie Obituary Louisiana. Avit Guidry and Sidonie. Avit and Sidonie Wedding Lafayette.* Nothing of use came through—they looked at the images, but there weren't any pictures related to Sidonie.

"She's done well in staying hidden," Charlotte said.

"I guess it's for the best," Aristide said.

"I'll keep looking for you, and I'll definitely let you know if I find anything."

"Either way—drop by anytime. You know the address."

"I do."

They hugged—he wanted to kiss her on the cheek.

"Take care, Aristide the Glide—I'll see you soon."

Aristide didn't go straight home from the library—he took a slight detour and headed over to Frog Creek Crow, where he had a favorite spot in the shade under a row of pecan trees. He took off his shirt and lay in the grass, the sun peeking through the branches. A few pecans were around him, and he cracked some against each other to eat. The long walks and the sun had gotten to him, and he closed his eyes—when he woke up, it was evening.

"Mom," he whispered as he gained his bearings. "Dad."

He found himself in a dark world again—his thoughts haunted him as they had done that one night in the kitchen. He took off his shoes, his jeans, stripped naked, and entered the water, kneeling down. The frogs were loud—the creek, in its rhythm—a song for anyone who listened. Aristide listened. He lunged forward face first into the water and closed his eyes. Flashes of his past seeped in. Clasping his hands, he closed his eyes tighter and held his breath for as long as he could. The water hushed the world for him. He pushed himself back up, breathing hard and loud. The frogs were still there. Aristide listened.

He walked home half naked, not going inside—he sat on the porch, pretending that his dad was there sitting in the chair next to him.

Just as the mosquitoes were making their way and as the sun came down, Aristide saw a shadow walking toward his house. He let the mosquitoes take his blood as he waited for the stranger to arrive. The sky was darker than usual, signaling rain.

Closer and closer. Aristide waited. He tried to make sense of the slow-walking person.

"Dad?" he said. "Dad?"

Soon enough he realized that the person wasn't his dad but a lady. She walked up, wearing a sunhat and sunglasses, though the sun was gone by the time she arrived.

"Hello, ma'am," Aristide said.

She took off her glasses and looked at Aristide, looking like she wanted to smile. Her voice was strong and vibrant.

"Sorry, honey," she said. "I'm a bit late."

Aristide looked at her eyes and lips and chin. He thought that she looked so familiar.

"I don't know you," he said. "But you look like someone I know."

"I know," the lady replied.

She turned around and looked at the magnolia tree.

"It's been a while," she said. "Looks like that tree needs a bit of mending."

Aristide looked at the tree and then at her again.

"Let's get you inside before the mosquitoes take your bones," she said. "The clouds are coming, too."

"Yes, ma'am," Aristide said.

In the kitchen, the lady took out the kettle and two mugs to make some tea. She knew where everything was kept. Only the sounds of the clattering and clanging of tin and porcelain and wood filled the room as Aristide watched in silence. She reminded him of his dad.

She sat down in front of Aristide.

"Mother," Aristide said.

"Son."

"Why'd you leave?"

"I know."

"Why?"

Sidonie rubbed her hands against the wood of the table.

"It's been really tough, you know."

"I'm here. I'm here forever."

"You're here, right?"

"I'm here."

She stood and walked over to the stove—the kettle was getting ready to whistle.

"We're here, Aristide. And we'll turn that magnolia back into magic, and we'll be okay."

"Yes, Mother."

The kettle started to sing, and Sidonie sang along—a lullaby, a lullaby that Aristide once heard before. And the rain started to come down.

JUSTIN PETER KINKEL-SCHUSTER

Filth and Time

A thing one is liable to forget
about the Mississippi
in absence from it:
its smell

clean and new
for all its aged murk
earthen, staid
for all its tireless endless
movement homeward
through filth and time

The *Industry*, 1838

IT WAS FEBRUARY and thin plates of ice flecked the Arkansas River, but ice wasn't the problem. Low water upriver was the reason Captain Anson Pennywit's steamboat *Industry* had been stuck in Little Rock for five days. Delays were common at that time of year, the river being unreliable even in the mildest winters, but on this trip Pennywit's cargo included nearly two hundred immigrating Cherokee, and now the water had finally begun to rise, the agent in charge of the Indians' transport, a blustering Georgian named Kincannon, was demanding he get underway immediately.

The boat's crew had scattered, however, and Pennywit spent the better part of a day tracking down his pilot. By the time he stumbled into Brown's Tavern, his nerves were so frayed he needed a long moment to spot W. J. Clark in the crowd. Clark was seated by the hearth, and he had a half-empty mug of beer in his hand, but—to the captain's great relief—he appeared, if not sober, at least not quite drunk. He was deep in conversation with four stevedores hunkered shoulder-to-shoulder around his table, though, and Pennywit had to pronounce his name twice before Clark stopped in midsentence and lifted bloodshot eyes to survey the room.

"This is unexpected, sir," the pilot said when he recognized Pennywit, adding with exaggerated camaraderie, "Make room for the captain, fellows, make room."

A space opened on the unvarnished bench, and Pennywit sat down as a wave of fatigue rolled through him. It left him briefly dizzy, his legs heavy as cast-iron stoves, and he waited until the room stopped reeling, then spoke slowly, testing his grip on his thoughts as he articulated them. "*Red Bird* arrived this morning, Mr. Clark. Her captain says the river is now open all the way to Fort Smith."

"Cholera?" Clark asked, frowning.

"Captain Tucker says not."

"Don't know a Captain Tucker."

Pennywit understood this was a lie. W. J. Clark had been a steamboat pilot on the Arkansas River for more than a decade, and it was his job to know its men and boats as well as he knew its hidden snags. Pennywit had employed Clark several times in the past year alone and had observed him to be both very good at his profession and sharply forward in his self-interest.

"I take Captain Tucker at his word," Pennywit said. Then, hemmed uncomfortably between two stevedores twice his size, he came to the point. "I want you to assemble the crew and make ready to depart before sundown."

Clark lowered his mug. "I'm not your mate."

"The mate is no longer with us."

"Debauched, is he?"

"I need you to assume his duties, Mr. Clark."

"Don't know as I can assist you, Captain." Feigning helplessness, Clark turned his palms to the smoke-stained ceiling. "I'm just a pilot, after all."

"I will double your wages for the duration," Pennywit said.

There was a sudden bark of laughter from across the room, and Clark tilted his head as though doubting he'd heard correctly.

"Double?"

Pennywit nodded.

"To act as pilot *and* mate?" Clark pressed, and Pennywit could see he was enjoying the goggle-eyed reaction of the stevedores.

"Until we return to Little Rock, yes," Pennywit said. Clark did not respond, so Pennywit felt compelled to add, "You know my crew. They are all free men, and capable. Your additional duties will not be arduous."

"Still, it's not really my line, is it?"

Although he had expected Clark to reject his initial proposal, Pennywit hesitated to sweeten it. *Industry*'s owners were being well compensated for their part in executing the federal government's Indian Removal policy, but they counted every cent and raged over unanticipated expenses. They might well fire Pennywit if Kincannon complained he was slow to get *Industry* moving again, but they were even more likely to do so if they judged he'd offered Clark too generous an incentive to satisfy the removal agent's desire for haste.

"Plus ten percent," Pennywit said after careful consideration, "but only upon successful completion of the job."

Clark leaned forward, elbows on the table. "Ten percent of my *doubled* wages?"

"That is my offer."

"Twenty percent."

Pennywit drew a breath of the tobacco-reeking air. "Not possible."

"Fifteen," Clark said.

"No."

"Full payment up front, at least."

Pennywit shook his head.

"Then . . . I don't think I can help you." Clark looked around at the stevedores, who, despite the depth of their inebriation, gaped at him as though genuinely stunned by his brass. Pennywit thought their regard emboldened the pilot, and told himself not to waver. "All due regret, of course, Captain," Clark added with false courtesy.

"I could find another pilot," Pennywit said.

Clark sat up straight at that. "You'd sack me?"

"It would take a little time and the new man wouldn't know *Industry* as well as you do, but we could be under steam by first light."

"I figure tomorrow afternoon at the earliest."

"Dawn at the latest," Pennywit insisted, though he feared Clark might be right. "Naturally, in the future, I will be inclined to seek out the services of the pilot here in Little Rock who is most helpful to me in this present difficulty."

Clark narrowed his reddened eyes to study Pennywit across the table. The captain kept his expression firm, not flinching when a bottle shattered behind his back at the bar. Clark waited until the ensuing uproar subsided, then cleared his throat. "Well," he said, "you're a fair man all in all, and I reckon we'll be seeing a lot more of you and Mr. Kincannon until the Indian trade runs its course. Let's meet halfway and call it done."

Now it was Pennywit's turn to clarify: "Halfway meaning nothing up front?"

There was another long pause, but in the end, scowling, Clark nodded. "And what, if I may ask, will you be doing while I'm making ready?"

This was not a question for which Pennywit had prepared an answer. Knowing he shouldn't respond, he heard himself say, "There is an important matter I must resolve before we depart."

"Ah," Clark said, the corners of his mouth turning up to form an anticipatory grin, "I wondered whether there was a young lady hereabouts."

The stevedores swung their bleary attention to Pennywit and he felt himself flush, his self-control temporarily depleted.

"I wondered," Clark went on, "because all this time, while Mr. Kincannon fussed and fumed about being detained here, you were in no hurry to continue our progress."

Pennywit rose, barking his thigh against the table. "You have work to do, Mr. Clark."

The pilot's grin became a full-fledged leer, and he raised his mug in a perfunctory effort to hide it. "Aye, aye, Cap'n. Aye, aye."

Pennywit hurried away from Brown's Tavern—trailed, he imagined, by knowing laughter from Clark's cronies. Overhead, dark clouds were massing, and there was a promise of rain in the wind whipping past the low wooden buildings jumbled along the river. He buttoned his coat and started up the steep muddy street, taking long rapid strides to dispel his fatigue. It was an effort that seemed likely to fail. During the five days *Industry* had been stalled in Little Rock, he'd gotten no more than a dozen hours' sleep, and none of them had been restful.

He blamed his sleeplessness on the always-present fear of disease, exacerbated now with so many people packed onto the idled steamer and its twin keelboats, but the truth was his worries went further. This was his first trip carrying displaced Indians to the west, and he'd found he despised the work. So much so that—as Clark had deduced—he'd secretly welcomed the closing of the river despite the not inconsiderable risks to his health and his purse.

In fact, he'd spent the past five days hoping Kincannon would decide to take his Indians overland to Fort Smith on the Cantonment Gibson Road. In the end, it was not to be. The agent was fifty years old, spectacularly fat, and plainly unwilling to undertake or even consider a long journey on horseback.

Pennywit was therefore left with responsibility for the entire party: his crew, his cabin and deck passengers, and the Cherokee who'd been crowded onto *Industry*'s keelboats. The Indians made him profoundly uneasy. They were a ragged mix of men, women, and children, and although their demeanor was overtly resigned, they watched Pennywit and his crew with a particular blank gaze he understood masked deep and abiding hostility.

Adding to his discomfort was the surprising discovery that, while a few of the Cherokee had something of the appearance of the Indian, many showed no sign of retaining in their veins any drop of aboriginal blood. Rather, the dispossessed emigrants huddled in his keelboats seemed mostly descended from individuals who'd intermarried with African slaves and even, in some cases, White settlers.

Mary Vann, though, had come from purer stock. Her gaze, when it found Pennywit's, had masked nothing. Now he felt a knife of anguish twist in his bowels—stumbled.

A teamster shouted at him, and Pennywit lurched up onto the boardwalk as a wagon loaded with raw timbers rattled past in the street. He gripped a wooden post, closed his eyes. Guilt assailed him, and had he eaten that day, he would have retched. Instead, he stood shivering, drawing quick shallow breaths, until he felt a tug at his coat.

Opening his eyes, he saw a dirty-faced, blond-haired boy of seven or eight. "You all right, Mister?"

Pennywit nodded wordlessly, and the child released his coat but continued looking up at him. The captain fished a nickel from his coat pocket and held it out. The boy didn't move.

"I don't want anything from you," Pennywit managed. "Take it and go."

The boy considered for a second more, then snatched the coin from his hand and darted into an alley. Pennywit stayed where he was. He still felt faint and needed time to catch his breath and regain his bearings. A single raindrop, cold and fat, struck the back of his neck. He glanced up at the sky and then around at the unpainted, dimly lit storefronts lining the street. Directly opposite him an enormous reddish-brown pig was tethered to a post. How had he failed to notice it earlier? It shifted slightly, blinking its small black eyes, and Pennywit saw that the animal was a sow. While he watched, she emptied her bowels in the middle of the boardwalk.

He turned away and continued up the hill. In his limited experience of the place, Little Rock was an extraordinarily filthy, often violent town, and until recently he hadn't cared to spend any time there. Six months before, however, while awaiting a load of overdue cargo, he'd sought out a Methodist church for Sunday morning services, and the episode had presented him with the prospect of a very different life than the one he'd known. It was not a religious conversion. Unlike most of the men he worked among, Pennywit was devout: He and his younger brother had been reared by a Methodist preacher in Knoxville, Tennessee, after their father abandoned them and their mother died of typhus.

What had happened in that small redbrick church in Little Rock was that he chanced to exchange a few words with the preacher's daughter.

Elizabeth Eaton was twenty years old, seven years younger than Pennywit. She was small-boned, almost doll-like, with fair skin, blonde hair, and astonishing blue eyes. Since their initial meeting, he had contrived, whenever his work permitted, to attend her father's services. During his most recent stopover in Little Rock, he'd received permission from Reverend Eaton to call upon her at home.

For the past five days, though, he had fought against the impulse to seek her out. He'd felt, for the first time in his life, unclean and even unworthy. He admired Miss Eaton for her beauty, of course, but also for her intelligence and moral clarity. That she was educated he had ascertained during their first brief conversation, and the novelty of discovering a refined and unmarried young woman in this rough river town was as transfixing as the perfect blue of her eyes.

Twice during the last twenty-four hours he'd set out for Reverend Eaton's house, only to turn back. He didn't think he could bear to shake the man's hand any more than he could look Miss Eaton in the eye. But with *Industry*'s departure now imminent, a desperate need to see her had overwhelmed his misgivings, and when Pennywit reached the top of the hill, he had to restrain himself from running.

Ten minutes later he stood in front of the Eatons's home. It was brick, two stories with bright white shutters and a steeply pitched roof. A waist-high iron fence separated it from its neighbors, which were larger and less carefully maintained. As he knew it would, it reminded him of the house he'd grown up in; it had the same scrubbed propriety, the same unassailable air of earthly permanence.

He opened the gate, crossed the small lawn of dead winter grass, and scraped the mud from his boots before mounting the porch. A Negro maid in a stiff black dress answered his knock.

"Captain Anson Pennywit. To see Reverend Eaton." The maid regarded him skeptically, as though she could smell the smoky reek of Brown's Tavern on his person, so he added, awkwardly, "I am an acquaintance."

"One moment, sir," she murmured, already withdrawing.

He remembered to remove his hat and pressed a hand to his stomach. There was one last impulse to walk away, but he stood flat-footed, holding his place through an effort of will.

"Captain Pennywit. What a grand surprise."

He started, realizing he hadn't heard Reverend Eaton's approach. He wondered whether he'd somehow dozed off because the preacher was a difficult man to overlook: tall and broad-shouldered, with a heavy, lurching tread that rattled a loose plank as he stepped onto the porch. Eaton's ruddy features and jet-black hair made him seem younger than his sixty years, and Pennywit thought again that Miss Eaton must favor her mother, whom he gathered had been deceased since she was a child.

"I regret the timing, however," Eaton continued, buttoning his topcoat, "as I am obligated elsewhere." The preacher permitted himself a small smile, and Pennywit understood his own expression must have fallen at the pronouncement. "My daughter will be nonetheless delighted that you've come. You always have such interesting news."

"I couldn't—"

"Nonsense. Marie is here," Eaton said, indicating the maid who waited just inside the door. "She will put on a pot of tea. Perhaps you would care for a late lunch?"

"I couldn't eat, sir, thank you. My boat is leaving for Fort Smith. I cannot stay long."

"Well, however brief it may be, Elizabeth will enjoy your company. I hope you and I will have the opportunity to visit more extensively the next time you stop in our town."

"Thank you, sir."

Eaton touched his hat and left Pennywit standing on his porch. The maid held the door.

* * *

"And *have* you interesting news?"

Miss Eaton spoke over the rim of her teacup, which she held firmly in one small unblemished hand. There was a faint flush in her cheeks, almost a suggestion of mischief, though she was attired as primly as ever in a navy pinstripe dress with a high collar and puff sleeves. Marie sat knitting in a corner of the parlor, a small room made smaller by the overstuffed bookcases that lined its walls. Pennywit took a chair facing Miss Eaton across a low table piled with even more books—volumes of English poetry, natural history, and Methodist theology.

"Miss Eaton, I—"

"Please, you must call me Elizabeth."

"I could not."

"I insist. And I shall call you Anson."

Pennywit blushed. "As you wish."

"So," she said, smiling, "what tidings of the world do you bring from your travels?"

"We have been . . . delayed for several days. I've not seen any recent newspapers." Looking into her eyes, aware of her expectant intelligence, he hesitated. "I was in New Orleans three weeks ago. There had been some slight improvement in the price of cotton, and sugar had advanced one or two cents per pound."

She nodded gravely, as though this information were of the greatest importance.

"And you," she said, "you have been well? I've heard there is illness in towns along the river."

"There is no sickness on *Industry*. We are very careful."

"I should like to see it someday, *Industry*."

Taken aback by her directness, he shifted uncomfortably in his chair. "The boat is in good order. However, my passengers at the moment, it would not—I would not—subject you to their kind."

"What can that possibly mean?"

"I am presently engaged in the business of transporting emigrants to the west."

She set aside her cup. "By 'emigrants,' you mean Indians?"

"Yes." Pennywit paused, distress roiling his gut once more. "There are about two hundred Cherokee in my charge. They are transported on keelboats, which slow our progress but have the advantage of keeping the Indians entirely separate from my White passengers."

He sensed fresh scrutiny and saw the maid staring at him from the corner. As soon as he turned his head in her direction, she resumed her knitting.

"Is that necessary," Elizabeth asked, "confining them in such a way?"

He wanted suddenly to tell her that many of the Indians could pass for White, but it was impossible to discuss with a woman of her delicacy anything at all having to do, even indirectly, with copulation, let alone miscegenation. "It's safer," he said instead, "for them and for my passengers. The keelboats are equipped with temporary shelters and cooking-hearths."

"Still . . ."

"The keelboats are of the largest class," Pennywit said, more sharply than he intended. "There is sufficient allowance for the health and comfort of the people."

Elizabeth raised an eyebrow. "I see."

He sat miserably. They were close to the subject that had compelled him to seek her company, but in the confusion of his feelings, he didn't know how to raise it.

The silence continued until she spoke. "Are you certain you wouldn't take a cup of tea?"

"Thank you, but no."

She turned to the window, and for a while it seemed to Pennywit that she was searching for something in the overhanging clouds. At length, though, she faced him again and explained that the winter had been unusually hard. "My father has buried nine of his parishioners since Christmas," she said. "We very much look forward to spring."

He nodded dumbly. The Cherokee on his keelboats were wrapped in thin blankets and old coats. Most were bareheaded.

"I am especially eager to see my sister," Elizabeth continued in a noticeably lighter voice. "She is married to a successful cotton factor in Memphis, and Father and I anticipate they will visit us next month. I have not seen Caroline, or her children, in almost a year."

"Children?" he asked reflexively.

"Two girls, ages seven and nine." She saw his surprise. "Caroline is ten years older than I."

Pennywit nodded again.

"Caroline has a lovely house on the bluff. From her back porch, one may watch steamboats passing up and down the river. Such a tremendous amount of traffic. It's quite fascinating." She studied him for a moment. "Something's troubling you, Anson. What is it?"

He glanced at the maid, who was concentrating with great determination on her handwork. "I run a clean boat," Pennywit began. "All of my crew are paid for their labor. I will not captain a boat that depends upon slaves for its operation. And I have never lost a passenger to accident or violence." He stopped abruptly, unsure how to continue.

"My father made inquiries concerning your reputation, Anson. He says you are a man of good Christian conscience and professional diligence."

He jerked to his feet and went to the window. A Negro woman in a gray cotton dress was passing along the street in front of Reverend Eaton's house, a basket of kindling in her arms.

Shame mingled with need in him. "There was an incident," he said, keeping his back to Elizabeth, "after we left the mouth of the White River."

"An incident involving the Indians?"

"Yes. One of them."

"A death?"

"Yes."

He knew she was watching him, waiting for him to continue, but he stood looking out through the spotless glass. The street was empty now, the bare trees black in the dimming afternoon light.

"I ordered *Industry* stopped as soon as the alarm was given," he said. "I sent a yawl to offer succor, but she wasn't seen again."

"What was her name?"

He turned toward her. "Pardon?"

"The poor dead woman," Elizabeth said. "What was her name?"

"Vann."

"That was her first name, or—"

"Mary Vann was her name."

He watched Elizabeth close her eyes and bow her head. Her lips moved silently, and he was too shocked to speak again until she had finished. "You prayed for her?"

"Of course," she said. "What happened to Mary Vann?"

It seemed then that she was in the room with them, standing just behind Elizabeth: a copper-skinned woman of middle years, not tall but straight-backed and adamant. She was wearing a wool broadcloth skirt over a man's trousers, a long cotton blouse belted at the waist, and a thin shawl pulled tight across her shoulders. Firelight played against the side of her face, which was hard and straight, with dark, almond-shaped eyes, steep cheekbones, and a wide, downturned mouth nicked at the left corner by a small crescent scar. She was looking straight at Pennywit, and he recalled her black gaze locking onto his as she boarded the keelboat for the first time. None of the other Cherokee had met his eye that day. She had frightened him then, and she frightened him now, though he could not say precisely why. Ghosts were childish fantasies, the figure before him no more than a daylight manifestation of the mental strain that had robbed his nights of sleep.

"Anson?"

He blinked, and when he focused his eyes again Mary Vann's apparition was gone. "We—we don't know what happened to her."

"How can that be?"

"She went overboard," he said. "It occurred at dusk, while the emigrants were preparing their evening meal. No one saw it happen, or so her people claim." He shook his head in disgust. "One cannot rely upon them to tell the truth."

"Why would they lie about the death of this woman?"

"The river was smooth at the time, and Mary Vann was in good health; the removal agent, Mr. Kincannon, vouched for it." He waved a hand impatiently. "There was no reason for her to fall. She may have been pushed, or she may have jumped." Elizabeth did not respond, and he struggled over what to say next. "Who can understand what goes on in an Indian's mind?" he asked, wondering, as he had every night since the incident, why Mary Vann hadn't cried out for help. "They don't think as we do," he said. "They don't value life as we do."

"They love their children, surely, and I've read they revere their elders."

Pennywit suppressed a shudder.

Elizabeth said, "Did you know President Washington said the Indians ought eventually to be full citizens? That was his wish for them."

"Impossible."

"They have souls, Anson."

"Mr. Langham, the Methodist preacher who reared me, disagrees. He says they are less than human, and incapable of improvement."

"I do not think you believe that."

He folded his arms across his chest.

"How many have died during this forced removal?" Elizabeth asked with startling vigor. "Men, women, and children who, had they been left to their own lands, would be thriving yet?"

"The Indians never 'owned' any land. They never improved it." He didn't know whether this was true, but added, "They were rootless savages." He glanced again at the maid, saw her gawping foolishly back at him. "White men needed that land. White men who are building our country."

Elizabeth did not reply but instead, she too sat staring at him, bold as a trollop.

"You are a woman," he said when he could contain himself no longer. "You should not trouble yourself to form opinions on this matter. It is a thing for men to resolve."

Finally, Elizabeth looked away. All the color had left her face, he saw.

This unbecoming stubbornness on her part was bewildering, and he didn't know how to answer it; he could not bring himself to apologize for chastising Elizabeth when he was so plainly in the right. The piercing need for reassurance that had brought him here, he realized with dismay, would not be met. For all her professed interest in the events of the day, Elizabeth was too sheltered, cloistered here with her dusty books and her doting father, to understand the world in which he must live.

The finality of it sent a wrenching pain through his gut. It was so sharp that Pennywit almost gasped, but he managed to control himself and keep his expression firm.

"I have to go now," he said, dropping his hands to his sides. "*Industry* leaves before sundown."

"Of course," she said evenly. "Marie, please see Captain Pennywit to the door."

The maid set aside her knitting and rose to her feet. Pennywit told himself not to speak, then said, "Perhaps I will be able to stop here again when we return from Fort Smith."

Elizabeth gave him a formal smile. "I am sure, if you are able, that my father would welcome your company."

His farewell was mumbled, awkward. The maid, standing close by, eyed him now with undisguised satisfaction, but he didn't have the wherewithal to reprimand her. A fading tremor ran through him, and in its wake all he could do was retrieve his hat and coat and follow her out.

On the front porch he avoided the loose plank and stepped down into the yard. The wind had died but the air was colder, and there would be sleet rather than rain within the hour. Pennywit buttoned his coat and went out through the iron gate and started down the street. At the corner, he stopped and looked back at Reverend Eaton's tidy brick house. While he watched, two pale hands appeared in the parlor window and closed the curtains. Behind the muslin a lamp brightened.

He would never be certain how long he stood there. Eventually, the sound of hoofbeats pulled his attention away from the house. A White man on a fine black horse rode toward him. His features were hidden behind a thick white beard and he stared at Pennywit as he passed but didn't speak. The sky, heavy and gray, leaned against the peaked rooftops, and Pennywit breathed in the frigid air, straightened his shoulders, and went on.

Descending the hill, he replayed his few brief encounters with the Eatons, from the summer morning he first entered their church and exchanged a handful of words with the preacher's daughter up to the present instant. It was good that matters had advanced no further, he decided—all parties would be spared embarrassment. Furthermore, he could detect no fault in his own behavior, and this was a great relief to him. He felt certain Mr. Langham would agree.

He could no longer picture Mary Vann's face, he realized. In his mind's eye he could make out only a blurred shape hunched against the keelboat's starboard gunwale. Then, as he turned onto a busy thoroughfare, his thoughts veered unexpectedly, and he saw instead his long-deceased mother standing on the boardwalk. None of the other pedestrians noticed her, but for a few dazed moments he believed his mother was solidly there before him and not simply a projection of his overwrought imagination. She wore the dress that had been her favorite, light blue with a lace collar, the prettiest dress she'd ever owned, and there was no sign yet in her youthful appearance of the disease that would take her life. The sight of her as she had been in his early childhood, so full of obvious good health, pleased him until he recognized the disappointment in her expression. He ducked his head and thought about that for as long as it took him to decide what he must do, then turned away from her and hurried toward the river.

Nettie

She went out in forsythia,
the yellow day bursting over fields once white
with cotton and ablaze with corn,
over the road buried in asphalt that leveled it,
but it's still breathing underneath, pure dirt, hard
as a working man's back, a road that follows
the earth's curve. The tall weeds walk
up and down, singing alongside, and I
was the girl walking with them,
telling stories to the wind.

Strange, I should have been sadder.
Grandma's laughter was always wanting out, would
tease her mouth into a grin but had to hold itself in
for the worrisome times, and she could worry better
than anyone in Morgan County. Storms, the boys
running moonshine, Aunt Mattie going blind,
and my mother, the beauty among brothers
with fire in her mind.

That morning was the last time I breathed
the simple air. There's no one left
to pick the small, sweet jewels of time,
strawberries from her garden.

I Feed Them Anyway

They're soldier-like,
prowling for food in gray jackets.
Weather beats them down
but they take on rain
and cold anyway,
starving and fighting to eat,
split-eared, tail-bitten.

When I was a child,
the cold went into my hands
feeling their hard fur.
My uncles shot squirrels for fun
and I prayed they'd come back
to the world I knew,
though it too was torn
from things you'd think
shouldn't touch a child.

I've tamed them
from the woods
to eat from my hand
and confess the indulgence,
my protest of nature's ban
against the dark, bright eyes
that let me in.

Frail Flowers

Why do I keep looking past these suns, so jubilant
in their rows, to the dying season? To what follows glowing
pinks and daisies bedded in loam, glistening rubies
soaked to the roots and worms turned up pulsing like veins?
Already the blooms loud with bees have folded.

And then to see his face in the window, fresh as morning,
his sturdy working hands angling and fastening,
each movement sure as he levels and trims, steadies
the house as it stands and takes on time, and slowly sinks.
The furnace rages, a sun that never sets.

His eyelids, petals that I love to kiss, why ashes?

Transit

(for Emily)

At the museum of old trains,
the ever-rusting graveyard bound
by a living stream and a heavy
humid drapery of weeds hung from pines,
you in your slim black mourning dress and boots
pick your way among the rubble
of metal bones and tracks, then stop to pose
for my picture on the fourth step of a wooden stairs
disjoined from what it belonged to,
and turn your head this way and that,
spilling your sunlit hair down one shoulder
then the other.

No Words

M Y EARLY MEMORIES were tinged with blacks and grays, prickly edges and cloudy insides. Out-of-sequence snapshots. A sense of sadness, not harsh or choking—vague—wrapped around me like an invisible coat. Unease floated in the air around me. A sense of something awry. I didn't know the words for it, and words were not offered to me.

The first four years of my life were lived in a 1950s Mississippi Delta town sitting on the side of Highway 61. Now I realize how simple my life was. One day gently eased into another. Until the small world around me began to slowly shift and crack. Subtle at first. No one talked to me about these changes. Perhaps the silence that encircled me was to protect me from the problems of my parents. Perhaps they thought I hadn't noticed, as I went about the business of being a child. But I wasn't spared, and I noticed. Voices from other places found their way to my ears as I covered my head and waited for sleep.

* * *

I sat very still in my small rocking chair, feet crossed, staring though the porch screen. The porch was small, at one end a swing too big for me. The narrow street in front of our shotgun house was deserted except for the large woman walking by holding a parasol against the sun's glare. She mopped her face with a white cloth and never noticed me watching her. She shuffled slowly by, crossing the train track, over and out of sight. My hands curving over the ends of the small armrests, I turned my head back and continued my solitary gazing. I could see part of the sky through the trees. The sun was now hidden behind gray clouds. It wasn't night, but it was getting darker. I felt a shadow of uneasiness without knowing the word. I got up and went inside, the screen door closing silently behind me.

I walked through the house and out the back door, forgoing the temptation to run through the sheets hanging on the line. I walked across the scrabbly yard and up Verline's back steps. She had lived in this house, so open to me, since my grandparents had still been in the shotgun—a Black woman who had always given me a place just to *be*. Her skin was pale white and mottled with brownish spots. Her hair was tightly braided in narrow threads. I walked through the tiny spotless kitchen, which smelled faintly of something fried.

"Dat you, Cee? Don't be gettin' on my clean sheets with yo' dirty feet. Come on up here."

I found her on the porch. I stood by her chair and we silently watched dust sweep down the street. We never talked much. We didn't need to.

* * *

I sat by my mother on our couch, as close to her warmth as I could get. I placed my small hand in her lap, my attempt at understanding what I did not. I knew this man—our preacher from the First Baptist Church. He spoke quiet words in our direction. Could I catch them so I could understand? Like butterflies, they eluded me. My mother was crying. I saw her face, the tissue in her hand. I didn't like the crying. It unsettled me. I wanted her to stop. Someone must be dead, I thought. Isn't that why the preacher comes? Wouldn't I know? Someone would be gone. And then I remembered. Someone was gone. But he wasn't dead. My father had reluctantly left our narrow, neat home because my mother couldn't bear the nearness of him anymore. The preacher left, with words of "prayer" and "help" trailing after him. Neither of us felt any better for his coming.

* * *

I sat cross-legged on the cool floor, turning the pages of a book with no pictures. Turning the pages, not knowing the words. I pushed it away. The fan made soothing noises and gently ruffled my wispy hair. The floor seemed to tremble slightly under Mary's heavy steps as she moved toward the tapping on the screen door's wooden frame.

A young woman with red hair stepped inside, looked around, and asked to use the telephone. She looked at me and smiled tightly in my direction. I knew her. I'd heard her name as it was wrung and ripped through my mother's hands and flung against the wall. I'd heard her name as it fell to the floor, was scooped up by my father, and put in his pocket. I'd heard her name as he'd unwillingly and sadly left my mother and me that day. I was slightly unsettled by her alien presence as I watched her. Why is she here, I wondered. To steal what remained of my father? I was glad when she left with her own secrets for coming, a private mystery. I returned to the book with no pictures.

* * *

The sky was white. The air was heavy. In the distance heat waves rose from the road stretching out of town. My hand sweated in Mary's as we turned and walked toward town. She watched me while my mother, a hairdresser, worked at a local beauty shop. Most days we strolled our familiar path. Mary stopping to gossip and complain to friends along the way, with me impatient for a very cold Orange Crush. We would pass the courthouse with its attached jail, and I would always look up to see the shadows of men staring down through second-story bars. I would tightly grip the brown hand gently pulling me along and look away. I had often felt a brush of sorrow for the shadows, but lately imagined myself as sad as they. But I remained silent—isolated in a world of grown-up grief. Aloneness seemed to follow and nag me where, before, the everydayness of my life had been a security.

* * *

My mother opened the back door of the Ford, and I climbed inside. The seat was itchy to my skin. I leaned back and dangled my legs nervously. Mama spoke to my uncle and slid into the front passenger seat, gently closing the door. As we pulled away from the house, I moved to the open window and put my arm out to catch the breeze. My mother glanced over her shoulder at me. Her eyes worried and dark. A small curve of her lips. I turned away, pulling myself up to look out the long back window at clouds that never moved.

We turned onto the highway, the town shrinking as the car gained speed. I pretended I could stretch my arms, grab it all, and pull it with me—but then my home was lost in the flat Delta distance, swallowed up by never-ending fields. I lay down and closed my eyes. The car was quiet with only the rhythmic clicks of tires on asphalt and the soft murmuring of Mama and her brother. The hollow space inside my chest grew bigger. Thoughts of my father and my longing for him danced in the space inside me: a slow dance . . . side to side . . . up and down, soundlessly. I'll never see my daddy again, I worried. The thoughts filled me up, yet I was empty. I said nothing. I was a child, and I didn't know the words.

PLATE 66

Ivory-billed Woodpecker
PICUS PRINCIPALIS.

CARRIE LEE SOUTH

Leaving the Nest: A Bird-Lover's Search

IN SEPTEMBER 2021, the US Fish and Wildlife Service announced its intention to officially declare twenty-three species extinct. This would be the highest number of species that have ever been delisted from the Endangered Species Act at one time. Hearing this news, I can't help but wonder what good it will do. These creatures will lose their federal protections, casualties of deforestation. Of these twenty-three ghosts, the Ivory-Billed Woodpecker looms largest in the hearts of naturalists and haunts my home state's swamplands.

Arkansas is home to the Buffalo River, the Ouachita and Ozark Mountains, bubbling thermal springs, old-growth forests, diamond mines, and millions of acres of rice farms. After a good rain, crystals sprout from the soil like glittering seedlings. I grew up feeling like my fellow Arkansans were unfairly pigeonholed as ignorant yokels. Truthfully, most of us are natural-born conservationists. Even the hunters have a deep respect for the land and what it provides. In 2005, we were finally known for something hopeful: our lush forests were the last refuge of the Lord God bird.

Local legend has it that the Ivory-Billed Woodpecker earned its nickname, the Lord God bird, because of the exclamation those lucky enough to see one can't help but utter: "Lord God, what a bird." It is a mammoth, prehistoric-looking feathered creature with a three-foot wingspan. The inky black plumage is cut through with a bolt of white, starting behind the bird's bright yellow eye and zig-zagging down its back like a racing stripe. The lower half of the wings appear to be dipped in white. Other than its larger size, the white on its wings is what differentiates the Ivory-Bill from its common cousin, the Pileated Woodpecker. That, and the bone-colored beak for which it is named. The males have a startlingly red crest, while the female's crest remains black but ends in a slight curl.

I speak about the bird in the present tense, because like many others, I hold out hope that it is still alive out there. We often don't recognize precious things until they are gone forever. If an enormous bird can glide unnoticed through the bayous for sixty years, what other secrets might our untouched landscapes be hiding? Perhaps we haven't completely destroyed things.

The Ivory-Bill makes its home in the primeval forests and baldcypress swamps of the American Southeast. By the middle of the twentieth century, most of these forests had been cleared. The Cornell Laboratory of Ornithology holds the only clear video footage remaining of the Ivory-Bill, taken in 1935. The film features a mated pair keeping watch over their nest hole. Their large, reptilian claws cling to the side of the bark as they dart their heads back and forth, tilting like metronomes, scanning the area for predators.

I watch the footage over and over. They look majestic and fragile, like a portrait made from stained glass. It reminds me of that eerie video of the last Tasmanian Tigers in captivity that turned my stomach as a child. Knowing that they're extinct, it's hard not to anthropomorphize the Thylacines as they pace up and down their cage, their expressive eyes seeming to plead for help. The Ivory-Bill is closer to home. The more I watch this last pair protecting their clutch of precious eggs, the more desperate I become. Why couldn't we save them?

In 2004, a kayaker from Hot Springs paddled along the Cache River through the Big Woods area of Eastern Arkansas. Something that looked like a pterodactyl darted through the cypress and tupelo trees ahead of him to perch. He was soon in touch with Tim Gallagher of Cornell University and Bobby Harrison of Alabama's Oakwood College, two respected and experienced ornithologists. Within days, the men were drifting through the flooded forest of the Big Woods. Suddenly, a large bird flew toward their canoe. Both scientists pointed and yelled "Ivory-Bill!" before the bird changed course and disappeared into the trees. Maybe the bird would have perched nearby and they could have taken a clear photograph if they hadn't shouted, but in an interview with NPR, Gallagher recalls, laughing, "You don't want to be the only one who sees a bird like that and not have a witness." He was right. Having two ornithologists corroborate the sighting is what made the world stand up and pay attention.

After a year of research in the area, in conjunction with the Cornell Laboratory of Ornithology, they published their findings in the peer-reviewed journal *Science*, officially announcing to the world that the Ivory-Billed Woodpecker was not in fact extinct and had been rediscovered in Arkansas. This was huge national news, but it had even bigger implications in the state of Arkansas. I live in Little Rock, the capital city, but even my "cosmopolitan" town is often considered country-fried by the rest of the nation.

Species formerly thought to be extinct are found fairly often, like snails and frogs and insects, but the rediscovery of the Ivory-Billed Woodpecker captivated our national consciousness. Perhaps it's because birdwatching is a hobby enjoyed by nearly sixty million Americans, and finding this bird was something akin to a confirmed Elvis sighting.

But why do birds in particular capture our imaginations? I'm sure it has something to do with the feeling that we're looking at a living dinosaur. A woodpecker has four-pronged talons with two toes in the front and two in the back to allow them to grip the bark of a tree. Songbirds have three toes in front and one in back for perching, but it's these zygodactyl feet shared by woodpeckers, parrots, and large birds of prey like owls that look so alien.

Whenever my parrot perches on my finger, I'm fascinated by his scaled toes with curved claws. I can't help thinking about that scene in *Jurassic Park* when Dr. Alan Grant terrifies a child by holding a velociraptor claw and describing this six-foot turkey slashing open his belly and spilling his intestines.

* * *

I became a bird owner out of a deep loneliness and desire to reconnect with the natural world. I moved to New York City in 2011 to work in publishing and to get away from the South. I felt that in order to be taken seriously, I needed to surround myself with culture and tall buildings. On one hand, I accomplished my goal: I worked at an agency in midtown Manhattan. What I didn't expect was to be surrounded by millions of people and rarely speak to anyone. New Yorkers always seem to be in transit, focused on their next destination rather than on the people around them.

For several years I lived in Flatbush, Brooklyn, an hour's train ride from anywhere, with dirty streets and liquor stores walled off with bulletproof plexiglass. My apartment ceiling leaked and black mold grew in every crevice. I could barely afford my half of the rent for less than 700 square feet, and my roommate was a hoarder. Trees were a rarity. I remember coming home from work one summer night and my eyes filling with tears at the sight of a firefly.

I found Birdcamp one afternoon as I walked down 53rd street. They had to buzz me in to the small storefront to make sure all the birds were contained before they opened the door. The railroad-style bird specialty store and boarding facility was a cacophony of squawking parrots. The owner, Brian, was a bird-loving savant with a penchant for painting tin Civil War soldiers, and he would refuse to sell if he didn't like the look of you.

I saw a small cage filled with small, pink chicks that Brian was in the process of hand-feeding. Every day after work for weeks I came by to visit the Rosy Bourke fledglings until they were fully weaned and Brian trusted me enough to sell them to me.

Jesse and Flynn came to live with me in my squalid apartment. There is a lot of guilt that comes with being a bird owner. They are wild things that need to fly. Dogs and cats are domesticated animals; birds are not. I think this is another reason why birds captivate people. They're prey animals, always darting from perch to perch, bobbing their heads with serpentine movements.

I never clipped Flynn's and Jesse's wings. Every morning, as soon as the sun rose, I let them out to flit around the room while I got ready for work. When I came home, I ran to free them again. I left music playing for them throughout the day because I knew that in their natural habitat they would be surrounded by noise (though it would be the buzzing of the Australian Outback rather than an iTunes playlist).

In the wild, Bourke's parrots are an endangered species. Jesse and Flynn are a soft, cherry blossom pink with yellow-tipped wings and flecks of blue above their nares. They would never survive in the wild; their bright color mutations would ruin any chance of camouflage. Wild Bourkes are small and brownish gray with a rosy belly. They blend in perfectly with the reddish Australian soil and acacia bushes where they forage. I tell myself I've saved them from the harsh wilderness and given them a better life than they could have had otherwise, but the truth is that they gave me a sense of purpose and a connection to the wild that my life in New York was lacking.

* * *

When the Ivory-Billed Woodpecker was officially declared alive in the Arkansas swamps, the small farming town of Brinkley, located just a few miles from the Cache River National Wildlife Refuge, saw it as an answer to their prayers. The nickname Lord God bird took on another meaning.

A resident told NPR at the time, "You know, you got to realize we're here in the Delta. We're right next door to the poorest county in the whole United States. And we have been wanting something, praying for an industry." Ironically, duck hunting is the city's main source of income in the months of November, December, and January, when the rice fields are flooded. Hunters worried about wildlife officials shutting down large swaths of popular hunting areas to protect the Ivory-Bill's habitat. But another resident pointed out that "this bird thing is going to be good the year 'round, and my business has already improved, like, twenty percent. Everybody's enthused." They welcomed the bird with open arms and took advantage of the opportunity to capitalize on the birdwatching tourists coming from all over the world to try and catch a glimpse.

The town erected an enormous billboard next to their I-40 exit, proclaiming "Brinkley, Home of the Ivory-Billed Woodpecker." Local restaurant Gene's BBQ painted a mural on the side of the building: "Home of the ivory-billed burger. The bird is the word." They sold T-shirts, woodpecker memorabilia, and of course the famous burger: two hamburger patties, mozzarella cheese, pepper, bacon, and a sesame seed bun. A large portrait of the bird in flight graced the wall. A local barbershop offered a woodpecker haircut for twenty-five dollars, where your hair is styled to a point and dyed fire-engine red, mimicking the bird's crest, with close-cropped sides dyed black and striped with white.

A gift shop called "The Ivory-Billed Woodpecker Nest" opened in town. The owner, Lisa Boyd, rented out other properties in Brinkley, but decided to turn the building space on Main Street into a souvenir shop that would hopefully turn more profit than rent, exclusively selling T-shirts, sweatshirts, buttons, artwork, books, key chains, and other items that featured the bird. Visitors to Brinkley were greeted by a huge neon sign with a full-color portrait of the bird, advertising the Ivory-Billed Inn. Rita Clements, local artist and owner of Rita's Art, began selling large wooden cutouts of the bird. She had been planning to move out of the state due to the struggling economy, but the woodpecker provided a new opportunity. Popular recording artist Sufjan Stevens wrote a song called "The Lord God Bird" based on interviews with people in Brinkley and their excitement about the bird's return. It was a hopeful time.

The problem was that the evidence of the Ivory-Bill was limited to one grainy video recording of a bird flapping its wings in the distance. It became infamous, jokingly referred to as the Zapruder film of the bird world. In their report for *Science*, Gallagher and Harrison analyzed the video frame by frame, pointing to the white undersides of the wings, a distinct feature of the Ivory-Bill that separates it from the Pileated. They also measured the tree the bird took off from and concluded that the wingspan of the bird in the video was too large to be anything else.

But of course, the longer the scientists went without providing a clear photograph, the more the skeptics came out of the woodwork. With recording equipment set up all over the wildlife refuge and running for months on end, how could they not get one single clear picture of the Ivory-Bill? People began comparing the sighting to Bigfoot, and it seemed as though Arkansans were once again the butt of the joke.

Many people claimed to have seen the bird, but it was always so fast that they weren't able to get a camera out in time. Interviews with the people of Brinkley and surrounding areas started to sound like folks talking about alien abductions. National media seemed to be winking and nudging each other with their elbows: "Yeah, okay, sure Billy Bob, you saw the woodpecker."

The Cornell Lab of Ornithology spent around one million dollars and another year searching the Cache River area before announcing in 2006 that they had failed to capture any definitive evidence and would be ceasing their efforts there and moving to other areas of the state. Scientists around the world erupted in snark and anger about wasted federal funds. The debate raged on. One woodpecker specialist described the efforts as "faith-based ornithology." Cornell had captured some compelling audio evidence of what sounded like the Ivory-Bill's signature kent call, a beeping sound like that of a plaintive bike horn. But without photographic or video proof, no one wanted to confirm the bird calls. Dr. Jerome Jackson, a professor at Florida Gulf Coast University in Fort Myers, told the *Arkansas Times*, "I think that maybe it's a reality check for the people of Brinkley. . . . I keep telling them, don't hitch your star to one icon, but to the ecosystem and all of its values."

* * *

I drive to Brinkley on a muggy Saturday in 2021, sixteen years after the Ivory-Billed Woodpecker made national headlines. It's an hour away from Little Rock, halfway between my home and Memphis on a long, flat stretch of I-40. There's not much to see along the way other than bare farmland—it's too early in the year for many of our crops. I'm hoping to find some evidence of what the Ivory-Billed Woodpecker once meant to the town of Brinkley. Perhaps artwork of the bird, maybe some ardent believers who can tell me about their own sightings. I desperately want some reassurance that the bird still matters. I'm captivated by its haunting kent call and the black-and-white footage of the birds at their nest hole.

As I pass the White and Cache Rivers, I keep turning my head toward the forest. Some completely irrational part of me thinks the bird might just flap past my peripheral, and if I blink I might miss it. I reach Exit 216 and notice that the "Home of the Ivory-Billed

Woodpecker" billboard is gone. So is the Ivory-Billed Inn and its neon portrait. I decide to stop by the Chamber of Commerce first to see if they have any information for me. I follow my GPS down some gravel roads, past small houses bowing under the weight of the years, until I reach "historic downtown," a single city block with scattered Western-style false-front buildings. Some are occupied while others are not only empty, but hollowed out. I park in a small lot next to an abandoned building that might have once been a gas station; now it's filled with an assortment of trash and destroyed furniture.

The streets are empty, save for mosquitoes swarming above puddles of standing water—one resident later tells me that in Brinkley, the skeeters mate with hummingbirds. I make my way to the front of the Chamber of Commerce, only to find a sheet of paper taped to the window:

NEW OFFICE HOURS
TUESDAY, WEDNESDAY & THURSDAY
10:00 A.M. – 4:00 P.M.
IF NEEDED ANY OTHER TIME, CALL AARON

There is no phone number. I wonder if everyone just knows who Aaron is. A woman spots me standing in front of the double doors. I tell her I'm looking for information about the Ivory-Billed Woodpecker and she cocks her head, squinting, as if trying to recall a long-forgotten memory, and tells me I might try the Central Delta Depot & Museum.

The building, located in a restored 1912 Union Railroad Depot, features exhibits chronicling local history. When I arrive, I find that it's closed indefinitely. No one in Brinkley can afford to volunteer as a curator, so the museum sits abandoned for the time being.

I realize I probably won't find anything official documenting the

Ivory-Bill's presence, now that so much time has passed, but surely I could scrounge up some artwork or old memorabilia. I know that the gift shop closed years ago, but I think those Ivory-Bill T-shirts and key chains must still exist. There are several antique shops on the historic downtown strip, so I walk back that way.

I enter the first antique store expecting to find paintings of the Ivory-Bill or some of the wooden cutouts that Rita Clements used to make. It feels like I've embarked on my own expedition to hunt down the grail bird. It turns out that searching for the bird's image proves just as difficult as trying to find the bird itself. I pass dusty shelves of children's books, old VHS tapes, and a neon New Kids On The Block fanny pack. The booths near the front of the store hold more upscale furnishings, and something tugs at my heart every time I see an image of a bird. I enter one booth with a series of artworks featuring birds hanging on the wall. My eyes dart from robin to hummingbird to cardinal, scrutinizing each portrait, looking for that black bird with white stripes. There are ducks everywhere. Each time I turn a corner into a new booth, there's a wave of fresh excitement, like I'm getting closer.

A woman walks in—the first customer in the hour I've been here—and I introduce myself and tell her why I'm here. She gazes at me, momentarily stunned, then says, "You know, it's funny you bring that up. I have an old poster of the Ivory-Billed Woodpecker at home, and I was thinking about getting it framed recently. For the memory."

I ask her what it was like living here during that time. She tells me that her three sons were in the public school system, and they had units of study on the bird. One day they were out in the yard and she swears they saw it. The boys had received cameras for Christmas from their uncle and they ran into the house to grab them, but by the time they came back outside it had started to fly away and they chased after it. "It was so fast. I understand why nobody could get a picture of it. We really wanted to, though." After a couple of years, everyone gave up hope. She fondly remembers how the town's economy had seemed to turn around. Then the bird left, and so did Walmart, and so did many of the residents.

I walk down the street to the next antique store and find the owner outside smoking a cigarette. I tell him I'm looking for anything to do with the Ivory-Bill and he chuckles. He says he hasn't heard that in a long time. He doesn't think they have anything, but I'm welcome to poke around. So I do. I scour every booth, with the same hopeful anticipation, and again I am let down. There are no woodpeckers here. I leave with an old bluegrass record and a small framed cross-stitch of a blue jay.

* * *

After keeping my parrots in my Brooklyn apartment for a few months, they began to get sick. I watched Jesse's tail bob up and down as he struggled to breathe, his beak yawning open, tiny lungs rattling. Flynn's left eye became red and swollen. He scratched at it constantly. Something in the air was irritating their sensitive respiratory systems.

I should have known that it had something to do with my leaking pre-war apartment building. Even getting "fresh" air from an open window wouldn't help much. I'll never forget the time I walked home through the city and came in to blow my nose, only to see that my snot had turned a sooty black from the air pollution.

Finding an avian vet was another challenge, even in a big city like New York. Once I did, I had to figure out how to transport the birds without the freezing cold weather making them even sicker. It was February with a windchill of -15 degrees Fahrenheit. I put Jesse in a small, plastic carrier, wrapped with layers of scarves. I stuffed a sock full of uncooked rice, warmed it in the microwave, then placed my makeshift heating pad against the carrier. I packed the whole bundle into my jacket and shuffled to the subway station.

The vet diagnosed him with Psittacosis and started a regimen of expensive shots. She was wrong, by the way. The shots didn't help, and I spent every bit of money I had trying to keep him from suffering. I tried to sell old jewelry because I could no longer afford taco meat, but even the pawn shop thought that my things were worthless.

The birds were the only thing keeping me company outside of work hours. I couldn't lose them. My job had become my entire identity. Days were repetitive cycles of waking at sunrise, subway commutes, and editing contracts line by line.

One afternoon, my dad called to tell me he had been diagnosed with Parkinson's. His hand had been tremoring for a couple of years, but he insisted it was just anxiety and refused to see a doctor. He assured me that he would start taking medication and the disease would slow down for a few years. I sat on the edge of the Bethesda Fountain and cried.

The people I loved were over a thousand miles away. My father and brother were both suffering from destructive neurological conditions. I was in New York to pursue a publishing career, but I was beginning to realize that the career success I craved would have to come at the expense of everything else. My roots were in Arkansas, and I was withering like a plant trying to draw water from soil that I wasn't suited for.

Federal Aviation Regulations only allow you to travel with one bird on a plane. I bought Flynn and Jesse a mesh backpack fitted with perches, rented a car that I loaded with my few belongings, and drove back home to Arkansas.

The birds haven't been sick since we've been here.

* * *

I head to the last destination on my agenda in Brinkley: Gene's BBQ. My GPS routes me to a building off the main drag, now called DePriest's BBQ. There's a mural painted on the side of the building that I presume once said "Home of the ivory-billed burger," but now it just says "The Roost." Ducks of all kinds float on the painted pond and fly across the brickwork. As I snap a photo, a car pulls up next to me. A woman steps out, a waitress getting ready to go in through the back door to start her shift, and asks me what I'm up to. When I tell her I'm here for the burger, she says "Honey, you're in luck," and tells me to go around front and she'll meet me inside.

It's an unassuming restaurant with wood-paneled walls, the kind with full rolls of paper towels set on each table. I sit alone at one of the small tables and the waitress I met outside comes over to hand me a paper menu. I find the closest thing I've seen all day to evidence that the bird had been here: The Ivory-Bill Burger, two five-ounce beef patties, bacon, and pepper jack cheese on a bun. She jots down my order and points over to a group of about ten people seated at a long table, picnic style. "You're here at the right time; the locals are here and they'll tell you everything you want to know." The group enthusiastically encourages me to grab my purse and head over to join them for lunch. Turns out they call that the "community table."

I meet Henry, Mike, and Linda, then Janice and John, a couple in their sixties who run the local funeral home*. John tells me Janice is the resident "bird-brain" and she laces her fingers together, leans toward me, and launches into what she knows about the Ivory-Bill. "This place has been sold, but Gene had a photograph of one of 'em supposedly, in flight, on the wall here at one time. Now, the

---

* The names of Brinkley residents have been changed.

game warden's son said he used to see the bird all the time; he just knew it was a honkin' big bird."

John interjects, "He just thought it was the biggest woodpecker he'd ever seen, you know? He didn't think too much of it."

The door chimes and Janice turns to the newcomer. "Hey there! How are you doing, Chuck? Good to see you. Come on around and join the group if you want." They hug and it's immediately apparent that no one is a stranger here. I think about my time living in New York, and how I would sometimes go to the church down the street on a Sunday morning, not because I was particularly religious, but because I knew that the group all stood in a circle and hugged at the end of service and I wanted to be a part of it.

Mike turns to me. "I wasn't living here during that time period. All I know is every time I would come over and visit, Gene's would be full of people from the National Audubon Society."

Janice rejoins the conversation to tell me, "They did discover a lot of things, and said this area was very, very rich, they had no idea." Everyone agrees that the best thing to come out of the Ivory-Bill craze was national recognition for Arkansas's abundant landscape. I tell Janice about my life in Brooklyn and the moment I was so moved by the sight of a firefly.

I ask Janice how many people live in Brinkley. "Down to 3,000, I think. When I was growing up, we were around 6,000. Beautiful, beautiful town. A beautiful town until Walmart came in. Walmart came in and killed all our little businesses."

The group groans in agreement and Linda says, bitterly, "And then they left."

Janice nods and continues, "My dad had a service station, entire company out on West 70, and he could go to Walmart and buy oil cheaper than he could buy it from his wholesaler. Which I never felt like was right."

Suddenly my Ivory-Bill burger arrives. They all chuckle when I exclaim "it's huge!" and watch me take my first bite.

John smiles, "Do you think it does the bird justice?" I don't know if it does, but it's definitely a damn good burger.

Now that the conversation has turned back to the Ivory-Bill, Henry, who has been quiet through lunch, tells me about his own experience. "I can remember seein' him out in the woods. Scared me to death, slipped up on 'im, he jumped out on me, it looked like a big albatross you know, huge. That's in the '60s. I just thought it was a big bird; I didn't know what it actually was."

Our waitress comes back around to see who needs refills; she knows everyone by name. She hands me a piece of paper. "Found this for you."

It's the cover from the old Gene's BBQ menu. A full-color portrait of the Ivory-Billed Woodpecker soars across the page past a forest of baldcypress trees. It's angled slightly so that you can see the white-tipped plumage across its wings. I realize everyone is looking over my shoulder.

Mike tells me, "He used to have that big piece of art, when Gene had the place, hanging on that wall." The waitress tells me I can keep it. I tell everyone at the community table that I've got to head back to Little Rock, and they say they hope to see me again sometime. They're here every day. John smiles, "Same time, same station!"

I head home with my treasure: an insert from an old restaurant's menu. Though it's only a painting, and I'm holding a blurry photograph of that painting color-printed onto a thin sheet of paper, I'm drawn to the bird's bright yellow eye. Finally, I've found the Ivory-Billed Woodpecker in Brinkley. At the bottom underneath the business hours and the portrait of the bird, in capital letters: WE BELIEVE.

In April 2010, Cornell officially ended their search for the Ivory-Billed Woodpecker in Arkansas. By 2014, the US Committee of the North American Bird Conservation Initiative listed the Ivory-Billed Woodpecker as "Probably Extinct." Many experts agree that we're in the midst of a sixth mass extinction. In the last fifty years, North America has lost more than three billion birds. "Gone the way of the dodo" is part of our everyday lexicon, thrown around casually as if it's a joke.

Small towns in America face their own kind of extinction. Like me, many college graduates leave their hometowns and flee to the coasts. Brinkley's mayor told NPR in 2005, "We're coming up on graduation, and that is, to me, a very sad occasion, because we're exporting these young people out, because there's not anything really primarily to hold them. You know, some will go off to college, but they won't return." In the end, the Ivory-Billed Woodpecker didn't bring jobs to Brinkley.

My own backyard teems with cardinals, chickadees, thrashers, and waxwings. Many afternoons I sit stock-still near the birdfeeder, a visitor in their space, admiring their plumage as they spring from branch to branch. I'm no longer a transplant. I came home to a place where my roots can grow and spread.

Arkansas has ten national wildlife refuges, including 67,000 acres in the Cache River area where we found the Ivory-Billed Woodpecker. Whether we officially proved its continued existence or not, many acres of bottomland property gained habitat protection as a result of the search. Birdwatchers from all over the world took notice of our rich and abundant landscape, and many endangered species still make their home here.

What good will it do to declare the Ivory-Billed Woodpecker extinct? We may not have definitive evidence, but surely we have enough reasonable doubt to protect their native habitats from further destruction. The US Fish and Wildlife Service recently reopened the public comment period on their proposal to delist the Ivory-Billed Woodpecker. Its official status still hangs in the balance.

The residents of Brinkley believe it was there. I want to believe it still is.

About the Authors

KATHY M. BATES studies creative writing at the University of Central Arkansas's MFA Workshop, where she serves as the managing editor for *Arkana* literary journal. Her work has appeared in *Necessary Fiction*, *Arkana*, and elsewhere. You can find her on Twitter and Instagram @hellokmbates.

JIM BEAUGEZ, a Mississippi native, has been published by *Rolling Stone*, *Smithsonian*, *Oxford American*, *Garden & Gun*, *Outside*, and other publications. He also contributed to the 64th Grammy Awards official program and created and produced "My Life in Five Riffs," a docuseries for *Guitar Player* that traces contemporary musicians back to their sources of inspiration.

JACK B. BEDELL is Professor of English at Southeastern Louisiana University, where he also edits *Louisiana Literature* and directs the Louisiana Literature Press. Jack's work has appeared in *HAD*, *Pidgeonholes*, *The Shore*, *Cheap Pop*, *Heavy Feather*, *Okay Donkey*, *EcoTheo Review*, and other journals. His most recent collection is *Against the Woods' Dark Trunks* (Mercer University Press, 2022). He served as Louisiana Poet Laureate 2017–2019.

CASSIE E. BROWN is a writer of long- and short-form fiction and essays. Her work draws inspiration from her childhood in rural Missouri, classic children's literature, and her experiences as a queer misfit. Cassie's work explores what is ugly, beautiful, and true about rural places and fairy tales. Apart from writing, she is a clinical social worker and a tea aficionado.

KATY CARL is editor in chief of *Dappled Things* magazine and author of *As Earth Without Water*, a novel (Wiseblood, 2021). Her writing has appeared in *The Windhover, Vita Poetica Journal, Belle Ombre, Across the Margin* (Best of Fiction 2021), *Presence: A Journal of Catholic Poetry, Evangelization & Culture, St. Louis* magazine, and *Genealogies of Modernity*, among others. She is pursuing an MFA at the University of St. Thomas (Houston).

LESLEY CLINTON is the author of *Calling the Garden from the Grave* (Finishing Line Press), a chapbook that placed second among books of creative verse in the National Federation of Press Women 2021 Communications Contest. Her poetry and book reviews have appeared in publications such as *America, THINK, Christianity & Literature, Mezzo Cammin, The Windhover, Reformed Journal*, and *Ekstasis*.

ELI CRANOR played quarterback at every level: peewee to professional, and then coached high school football for five years. These days, he's traded in the pigskin for a laptop, writing from Arkansas, where he lives with his wife and kids. Eli's novel *Don't Know Tough* was awarded the Peter Lovesey First Crime Novel Contest and was published by Soho Press in 2022.

SHOME DASGUPTA is the author of ten books, including *The Seagull and the Urn* (HarperCollins India), *Spectacles* (Word West Press), and a poetry collection, *Iron Oxide* (Assure Press). Forthcoming novels include *Cirrus Stratus* (Spuyten Duyvil), *Tentacles Numbing* (Thirty West), and *The Muu-Antiques* (Malarkey Books). His writing has appeared in *McSweeney's Internet Tendency, Hobart, New Orleans Review, X-R-A-Y, American Book Review, New Delta Review, Magma Poetry*, and elsewhere. He is the series editor of the Wigleaf Top 50. He lives in Lafayette, Louisiana, and can be found at www.shomedome.com and @laughingyeti.

GEFFREY DAVIS is the author of *Night Angler* (BOA Editions, 2019), winner of the 2018 James Laughlin Award, and *Revising the Storm* (BOA Editions, 2014), which received the 2013 A. Poulin, Jr. Poetry Prize. His other honors include the Anne Halley Poetry Prize, the Dogwood Prize in Poetry, the Leonard Steinberg Memorial/Academy of American Poets Prize, and the Wabash Prize for Poetry, as well as fellowships from Cave Canem, the National Endowment for the Arts, and Penn State's Institute for the Arts and Humanities. He teaches at the University of Arkansas and The Rainier Writing Workshop and lives in Fayetteville, Arkansas.

HEATHER DOBBINS is a native of Memphis, Tennessee. She is the author of two poetry collections, *In the Low Houses* (2014) and *River Mouth* (2017), both from Kelsay Press. Her flash fiction and poems have been published in *Beloit Poetry Journal*, *Book of Matches*, *Channel*, and *Women's Studies Quarterly*, among others. She lives in Fort Smith, Arkansas, with her husband and their three sons. Please see heatherdobbins.net for more.

WILL JUSTICE DRAKE lives in north Alabama, where he teaches English literature and coaches soccer. He spent much of his childhood traveling to Tulsa despite I-40 construction in Arkansas. His poems and articles have appeared in the *Dead Mule School of Southern Literature*, *Flyway*, *Trinity House Review*, *Poetry South*, *Raleigh Review*, and other publications. He received his MFA from North Carolina State University. Twitter: @thewilljustice.

RENEE EMERSON is a homeschooling mom of seven, and the author of *Church Ladies* (forthcoming from Fernwood Press),

Threshing Floor (Jacar Press, 2016), and *Keeping Me Still* (Winter Goose Publishing, 2014). Her poetry has been published in *Cumberland River Review*, *The Windhover*, and *Poetry South*. She adjunct teaches online for Indiana Wesleyan University, and blogs about poetry, grief, and motherhood at www.reneeemerson.com.

ELISHEVA FOX is a mother, lawyer, and writer. She braids her late-blooming queerness, Texan sensibilities, and faith into poetry. Some of her other pieces can be found in *Brazos River Review*, *Susurrus*, and *Cordella Magazine*.

MELISSA M. FRYE, Arkansas native, reflects on life experiences to craft realistic fiction and poetry. Her writing career began with nonfiction in the form of book reviews for AOL and subsequently a weekly movie review column in a local newspaper. She has won multiple awards for poetry and short stories. When not writing, Melissa collects weird facts and useless information. For example, she knows why the giraffe's tongue is black.

CHRISTIAN ANTON GERARD is the author of *Holdfast* (C&R Press) and *Wilmot Here, Collect for Stella* (WordTech). He's received Bread Loaf Writers' Conference scholarships and the Iron Horse Literary Review's Discovered Voices Award. His work appears in places such as *The Rumpus*, *Post Road*, *The Adroit Journal*, *Diode*, *Ruminate*, and *Tupelo Quarterly*. Gerard is an associate professor in the creative writing program at the University of Arkansas–Fort Smith.

KRISTEN GRACE became a poet at age eight as a preacher's kid, reading the Bible for fun when she had no other books to read. She credits *Song of Solomon* with teaching her how to write an unusual love poem. Grace is a journalist for *405 Magazine*, a freelance copyeditor for Callisto Media, and a graduate student at Oklahoma City University's Red Earth MFA program. She has authored a children's book and a short story collection with Literati Press in Oklahoma City, and has a new poem in *Focus Magazine* (March 2022). In her downtime, she reads. And reads. And reads.

TAYLOR GREENE is an archaeologist living in Arkansas, so he spends more time reading in an office than you'd think. When he's not there, he's taking long drives to see archaeological sites and hunt for good barbecue. His favorite flower is the goldenrod, and his favorite bookstore is Square Books in Oxford, Mississippi. His work is in *Glitchwords, cool rock repository, The Brazos River Review*, and forthcoming in *Hell Is Real: A Midwestern Gothic Anthology*.

CAROLYN GUINZIO is the author of seven collections. *A Vertigo Book* (The Word Works, 2021) won the Tenth Gate Prize. Earlier books include *Ozark Crows* (Spuyten-Duyvil, 2018) and *Spoke & Dark* (Red Hen, 2012), winner of the To the Lighthouse/A Room of Her Own Prize. Her work has appeared in *Poetry, The Nation*, the *New Yorker*, and many other journals. She lives just outside Fayetteville, Arkansas. Her website is carolynguinzio.tumblr.com.

BRYAN HURT is the author of *Everyone Wants to Be Ambassador to France*, which won the Starcherone Prize for Innovative Fiction, and editor of *Watchlist: 32 Stories by Persons of Interest* (*Catapult*). His writing has appeared in *Lit Hub, Electric Literature*, and *TriQuarterly*, among many others, and has been translated into several languages. He is editor in chief of the *Arkansas International* and teaches in the MFA program at the University of Arkansas.

DEWAYNE KEIRN lives in northwest Arkansas and enjoys trips into the Ozark hills, where the scenery is both relaxing and inspiring. He has been published in *Sin Fronteras Journal, Cross-winds Poetry Journal, Xavier Review*, and *OzarksWatch Magazine*.

EMILY KEY lives in Savannah, Georgia. She is an educator, prefers musicals over plays, loves deeply, treasures her family, and cooks against her will. She enjoys reading and history and reading about history. She's an artist sometimes. Her work has appeared in *Free Flash Fiction*.

JUSTIN PETER KINKEL-SCHUSTER lives in Fayetteville, Arkansas, with his wife and their three dogs. He writes and records songs in multiple projects and releases those recordings via his record label, Constant Stranger.

TIMOTHY KLEISER is a writer and teacher from Louisville, Kentucky. His writing has appeared in *Atlanta Review, National Review, Modern Age, Still, Fathom, Front Porch Republic*, and elsewhere. He is an MFA candidate in poetry at the University of St. Thomas in Houston, Texas.

LAURIE MARSHALL is a writer and artist working in Northwest Arkansas. Recent stories have been awarded the 2021 Lascaux Flash Fiction Prize, included in the 2022 Bath Flash Fiction Award anthology, and nominated for Best Small Fictions 2022. She reads for *Fractured Lit* and *Longleaf Review*. Words and art have been published in *New World Writing, Rejection Letters, Emerge Literary Journal, Versification, Bending Genres*, and *Flash Frog* among others. Connect on Twitter @LaurieMMarshall.

BRYAN MOATS lives in rural Arkansas with his family of five. He is a farmer, illustrator, volunteer firefighter, writer, and former editorial art director for the *Arkansas Times*. Find Bryan on Twitter @BryanMoats or Instagram @brynomite.

SCOTT MORRIS has a Master of Fine Arts in Creative Writing from the University of Arkansas and has published short fiction in the *Texas Review* and other journals. He has worked as a newspaper reporter in three Southern states and done stints in politics, international development, and corporate communications.

BENJAMIN MYERS was the 2015-2016 Poet Laureate of the State of Oklahoma and is the author of three books of poetry: *Black Sunday* (Lamar University Press, 2018), *Lapse Americana* (New York Quarterly Books, 2013) and *Elegy for Trains* (Village Books Press, 2010). He has also published one book of criticism, *A Poetics of Orthodoxy* (Cascade Books, 2020). His poems may be read in the *Yale Review*, *Rattle*, *32 Poems*, *Image*, *Nimrod*, and other literary journals. He has been honored with an Oklahoma Book Award from the Oklahoma Center for the Book and with a Tennessee Williams Scholarship from the Sewanee Writers' Conference. His prose appears in *World Literature Today*, *Books and Culture*, *First Things*, and other magazines. Myers teaches at Oklahoma Baptist University, where he is the Crouch-Mathis Professor of Literature.

TODD OSBORNE is a poet and educator originally from Nashville, Tennessee. His poems have previously appeared in *Scrawl Place*, *EcoTheo Review*, *Tar River Poetry*, the *Missouri Review*, and elsewhere. He is a poetry reader for *Memorious* and a feedback editor for *Tinderbox Poetry Journal*. He lives and writes in Hattiesburg, Mississippi, with his wife and their cat.

SUZANNE UNDERWOOD RHODES is Arkansas' new poet laureate, appointed for a four-year term by Gov. Hutchinson on

January 27, 2022. She lives in Fayetteville with her husband, Wayne Rhodes, a landscape photographer, and is the author of several books of poetry and lyrical prose, including her most recent, *Flying Yellow: New and Selected Poems*, *Hungry Foxes*, and others. She also wrote a popular textbook, *The Roar on the Other Side: A Guide for Student Poets*. Her poems appear frequently in journals, books, and anthologies such as *Slant*, *Image*, *Alaska Quarterly Review*, *Christian Century*, *Words and Quilts*, and others. She has received many awards for her poems, including first place in the Virginia Highlands Creative Writing Contest. Suzanne teaches virtual poetry workshops through the Muse Writers Center in Norfolk, Virginia, and has an MA degree in poetry from Johns Hopkins University.

WHITNEY RIO-ROSS is the author of the chapbook *Birthmarks* (Wipf & Stock) and poetry editor at *Fare Forward*. Her poetry has appeared in *America*, *New South*, *Presence Journal*, and elsewhere. She lives with her husband and pup in Nashville, Tennessee.

C. T. SALAZAR is a Latinx poet and librarian from Mississippi. He's the author of *Headless John the Baptist Hitchhiking* (Acre Books, 2022) as well as three previous chapbooks, most recently *American Cavewall Sonnets* (Bull City Press, 2021). His most recent poems have appeared or are forthcoming in *Gulf Coast*, *West Branch*, *Southeast Review*, the *Hopkins Review*, *Pleiades*, *Ocean State Review*, and elsewhere.

GERRY SLOAN is a retired music professor living in Fayetteville, Arkansas. His collections include *Paper Lanterns* (Half Acre Press, 2011) and *Crossings: A Memoir in Verse* (Rollston Press, 2017), plus five chapbooks, including one in Mandarin. Recent work has appeared in *Cantos*, *Nebo*, *Slant*, *Xavier Review*, *Elder Mountain* (featured poet), *Cave Region Review* (featured poet), and *Plants & Poetry Journal.*

TYLER JUSTIN SMOTHERS is an Oklahoman, born and raised. His primary influences are the Cherokee author Diane Glancy, along with the Catholic literary tradition, with its particular expressions in Dante, Hopkins, and Toni Morrison. He lives with his wife in Oklahoma City, where he teaches writing and Medieval history and literature at The Academy of Classical Christian Studies.

CARRIE LEE SOUTH is an MFA candidate at the University of Central Arkansas, where she serves as the fiction editor for *Arkana.* Her work has appeared in *The Hunger, Halfway Down the Stairs, Incendium,* and elsewhere.

CASEY SPINKS is a doctoral student in theology at Baylor University, in Waco, Texas. He is a native of Baton Rouge, Louisiana.

HOLLY A. STOVALL has published short fiction, personal essays, literary histories, literary criticism, and scholarly research in *Writers Resist, Litbreak Magazine, Letras Hispanas, Peace and Change, In These Times, Inside Higher Ed*'s "University of Venus Blog," Tri States Public Radio, and the *Australian Journal of Environmental Education.* She holds a PhD in Spanish literature, an MA in Women's History, and is currently an MFA candidate in creative writing at Northwestern University. She lives in rural Illinois.

BUD STURGUESS was born in the oil and cotton town of Seminole, Texas. He has lived in Amarillo since 2008. Recent work has included *Sick Things* (a novel) and *Balladmonger: More Bad Poems and Prose.* Find him on Twitter @Sturgesverses.

GLORIA WILLIAMS TRAN grew up in California but has spent most of her life in western Arkansas. After moving to Paris, Arkansas, she worked as a radio deejay before earning her master's degree at UCA in Conway. Gloria taught for thirty-six years in Paris and Fort Smith. Her poetry has been published in *Gathering Storm*, *Do South*, *@Urban*, and an anthology by Poets' Choice. She recently received an award from the Poetry Society of Virginia.

MADELINE TROSCLAIR is a poet from Southeast Louisiana pursuing a masters of English in creative writing at the University of Louisiana at Lafayette. With an emphasis on ecological poetry, her work has been featured in *Susurrus*; *The Tide Rises, The Tide Falls* journal; *Tilted House*; and *EcoTheo Review*. She is fond of muddy rivers, garlic, and warm light.

SETH WIECK's stories, essays, and poetry have been published in magazines such as *Narrative Magazine*, *Front Porch Republic*, and the *Broad River Review*, where he won the Ron Rash Award in Fiction. Most recently a series of his poems were included in the *Lone Star Poetry* anthology, which benefits the hunger relief organization Feeding Texas. He lives in Amarillo with his wife and three children.

Acknowledgments

The following works appear here with the permission of their original publishers.

Jack B. Bedell, "Swamp Thing Ruminates on a Line from Thomas Merton," *Cheap Pop*, November 2021.

Katy Carl, "Fragile Objects," *Vita Poetica*, Spring 2021.

Lesley Clinton, "Grief's Handiwork: An Allegory," *Reformed Journal*, February 2022.

Geffrey Davis, "Arkansas Aubade" and "Pleasures of Place" from *Night Angler*. © 2019 Geffrey Davis. Reprinted with the permission of The Permissions Company, LLC, on behalf of BOA Editions, Ltd., boaeditions.org.

Geffrey Davis, "It is no small thing to discover fresh words for old wounds," *Poetry Northwest*, March 2018.

Bryan Hurt, "Brain in a Jar," *No Contact*, no. 21 (June 2021).

Timothy Kleiser, "Backyard Theology," *Fathom*, August 2019.

Bryan Moats, "Hanging the Bat House," *Moist Poetry Journal*, April 2021.

Benjamin Myers, "Decoration Day," *Oklahoma Today*, January/February 2017.

Suzanne Underwood Rhodes, "Nettie" and "I Feed Them Anyway," from *Flying Yellow* by Suzanne Underwood Rhodes. © 2021 Suzanne Underwood Rhodes. Used by permission of Paraclete Press, www.paracletepress.com.

Scripture quotation is from the Revised Standard Version of the Bible, © 1946, 1952, and 1971 National Council of the Churches of Christ in the United States of America. Used by permission. All rights reserved worldwide.

Images

cover: Railroad right of way map #619, "The Kansas City Southern Ry. Plan Showing Ground to be Leased at Spiro, I.T.," US Department of the Interior, Office of Indian Affairs, Five Civilized Tribes Agency, 1907. In the collection of the National Archives and Record Administration (via Wikimedia Commons).

p. 6: "Illustration of sliced apples" (via Pixabay).

p. 24: "Delta," Pearson Scott Foresman (via Wikimedia Commons).

p. 45: "Daffodil," Pearson Scott Foresman (via Wikimedia Commons).

p. 61: "Screech owl," Pearson Scott Foresman (via Wikimedia Commons).

p. 68: "Pitcher jug," Pearson Scott Foresman (via Wikimedia Commons).

p. 94: "Ink mushrooms" (1915) by Julie de Graag (1877–1924). Original from the Rijksmuseum, Amsterdam (via rawpixel).

p. 108: "Goldenrod," Pearson Scott Foresman (via Wikimedia Commons).

p. 114: "Winter," (1920) Julie de Graag (1877–1924). Original from the Rijksmuseum, Amsterdam (via rawpixel).

p. 116: "Hog," Pearson Scott Foresman (via Wikimedia Commons).

p. 134: "Rail," Pearson Scott Foresman (via Wikimedia Commons).

p. 143: "Two crayfish," Julie de Graag (1877–1924). Original from the Rijksmuseum, Amsterdam (via rawpixel).

p. 149: "Hazelworm," Julie de Graag (1877–1924). Original from the Rijksmuseum, Amsterdam (via rawpixel).

p. 171: "Stratus," Pearson Scott Foresman (via Wikimedia Commons).

p. 174: "Interchange," Pearson Scott Foresman (via Wikimedia Commons).

p. 191: "Stepladder," Pearson Scott Foresman (via Wikimedia Commons).

p. 196: "Shell," (1921) Julie de Graag (1877–1924). Original from the Rijksmuseum, Amsterdam (via rawpixel).

p.212: "Lizard," Julie de Graag (1877–1924). Original from the Rijksmuseum, Amsterdam (via rawpixel).

p.231: "Portrait of a woman," Julie de Graag (1877–1924). Original from the Rijksmuseum, Amsterdam (via rawpixel).

p. 241: "Rocking chair," Pearson Scott Foresman (via Wikimedia Commons).

p. 242: "Ivory-billed Woodpecker," from *Birds of America* (1827) by John James Audubon, etched by William Home Lizars. Original from University of Pittsburg. (via rawpixel).

Mid/South Anthology features forty talented writers from Arkansas, Oklahoma, Texas, Louisiana, and other surrounding states that represent a unique part of American culture. While this region is often misunderstood as one type of place, the Mid-South belongs to a little bit of everywhere: part Southwest, part Midwest, part South—always wild. Our area of the country is both a space of its own and part of a larger, complicated Southern world: the "Mid/South." In this collection, poetry, short stories, and essays offer glimpses into this in-between place as they explore the complexities of our relationships to each other as well as to the natural world. Whether through vivid landscapes, family dramas, or bittersweet love stories, each piece brings more insight into what it means to be from around here.

This is the first publication by Belle Point Press, a new independent small press based in Fort Smith, Arkansas. Our mission is to celebrate the literary culture of the American Mid-South: all its paradoxes and contradictions, all the ways it gets us home.

BELLE POINT PRESS
Fort Smith, Arkansas
www.bellepointpress.com